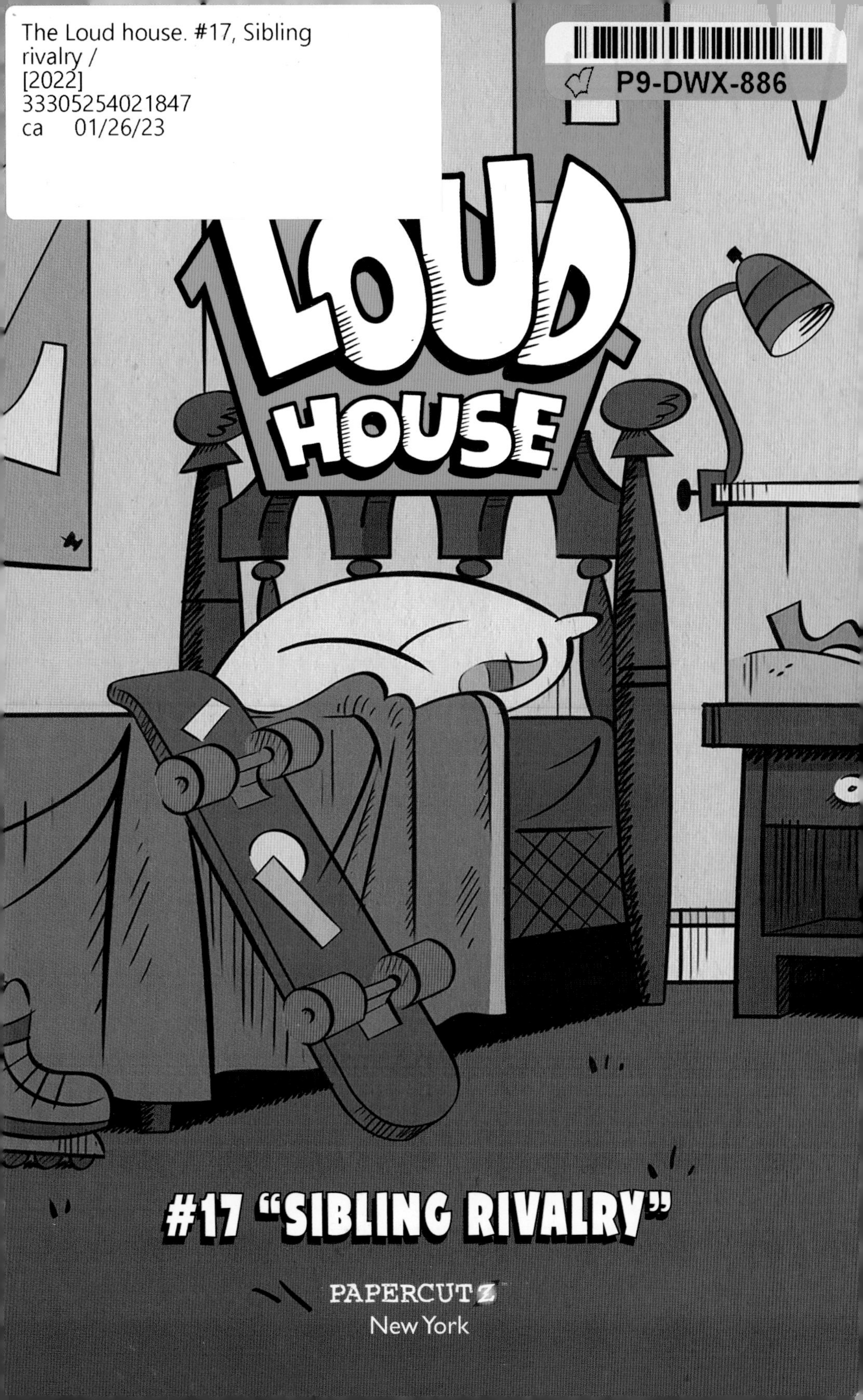

LOUD HOUSE

#17 "SIBLING RIVALRY"

PAPERCUTZ
New York

MORE GREAT GRAPHIC NOVEL SERIES AVAILABLE FROM PAPERCUTZ™

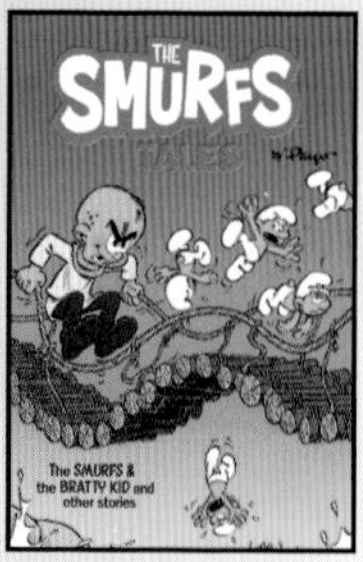
THE SMURFS TALES
The SMURFS & the BRATTY KID and other stories
THE SMURFS TALES

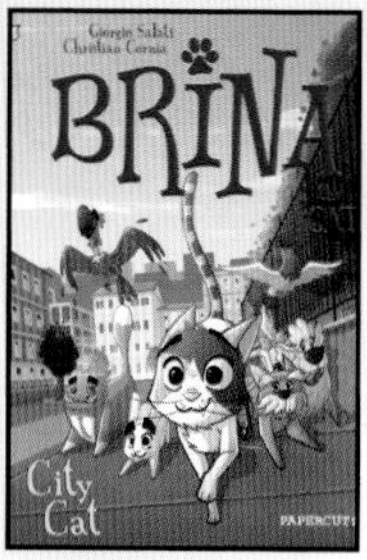
BRINA
City Cat
BRINA THE CAT

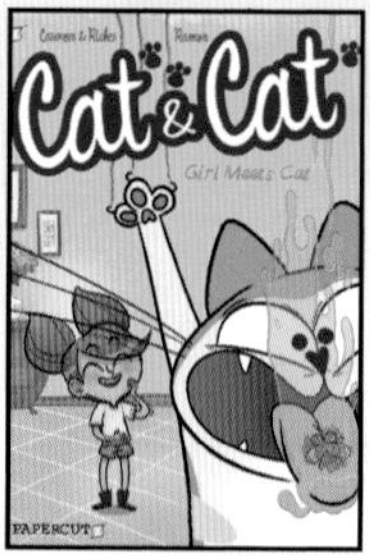
Cat & Cat
Girl Meets Cat
CAT & CAT

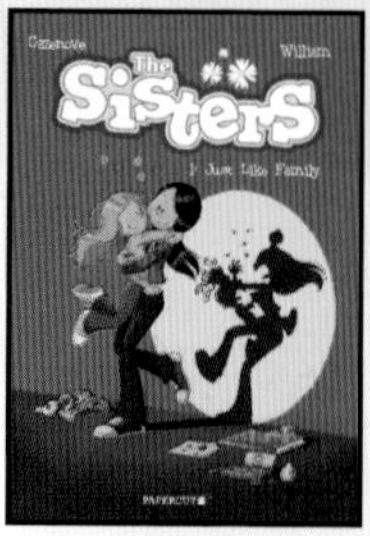
The Sisters
THE SISTERS

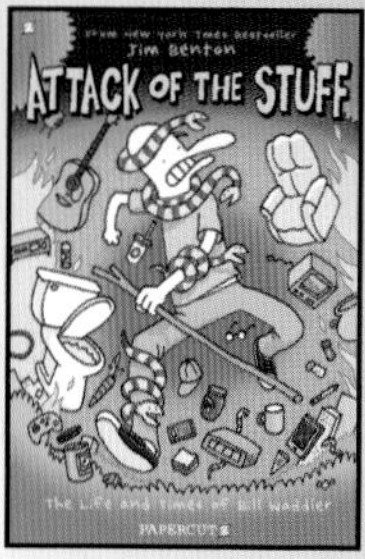
Jim Benton
ATTACK OF THE STUFF
ATTACK OF THE STUFF

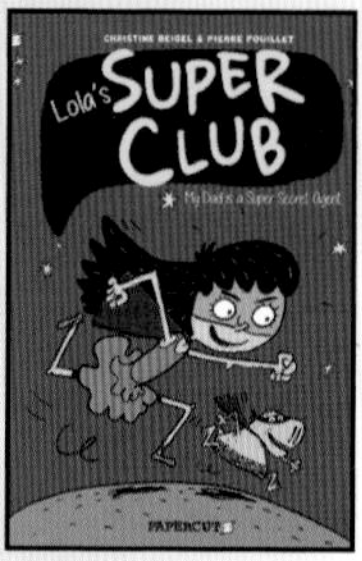
CHRISTINE BEIGEL & PIERRE FOUILLET
Lola's SUPER CLUB
LOLA'S SUPER CLUB

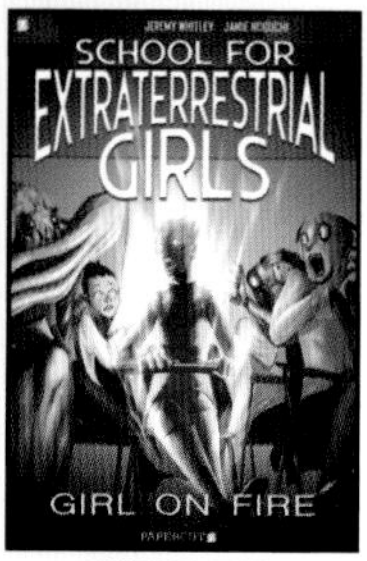
SCHOOL FOR EXTRATERRESTRIAL GIRLS
GIRL ON FIRE
SCHOOL FOR EXTRATERRESTRIAL GIRLS

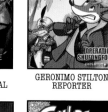

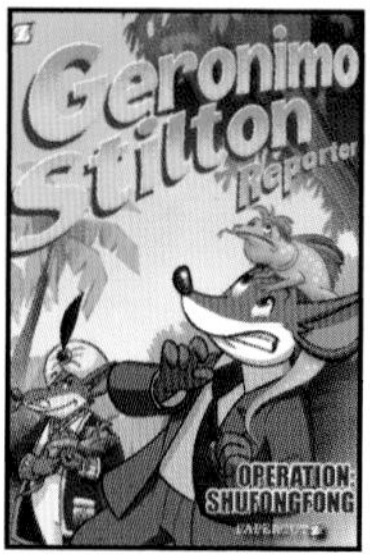
Geronimo Stilton Reporter
OPERATION: SHUFONGFONG
GERONIMO STILTON REPORTER

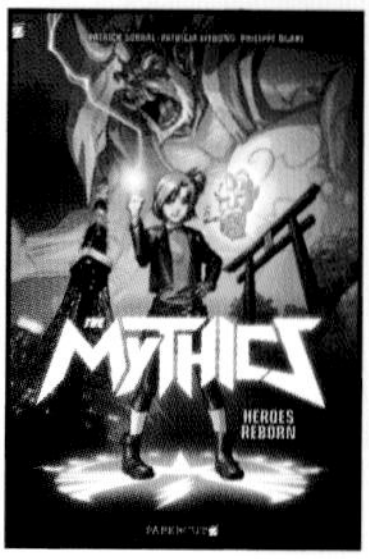
MYTHICS
HEROES REBORN
THE MYTHICS

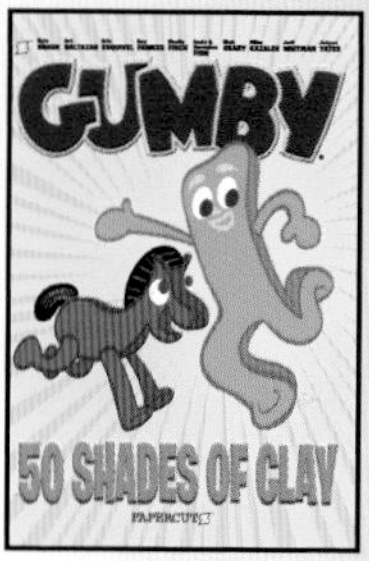
GUMBY
50 SHADES OF CLAY
GUMBY

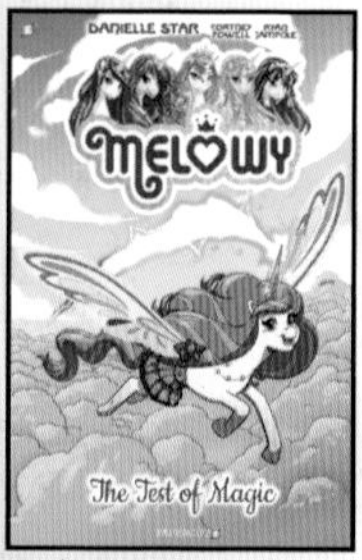
DANIELLE STAR
MELOWY
The Test of Magic
MELOWY

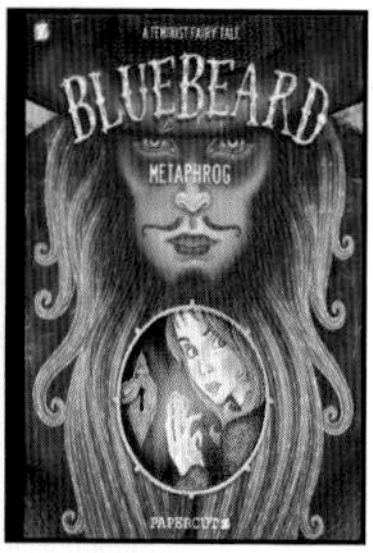
A FEMINIST FAIRY TALE
BLUEBEARD
METAPHROG
BLUEBEARD

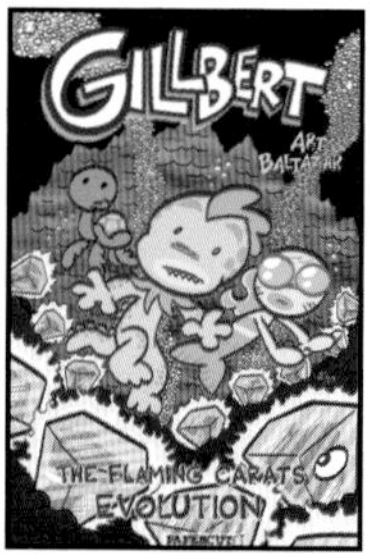
GILLBERT
THE FLAMING CARATS EVOLUTION
GILLBERT

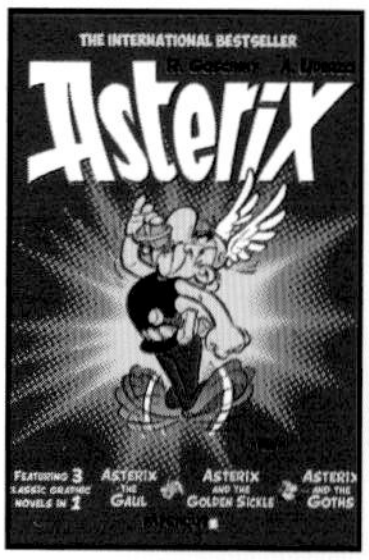
THE INTERNATIONAL BESTSELLER
Asterix
ASTERIX

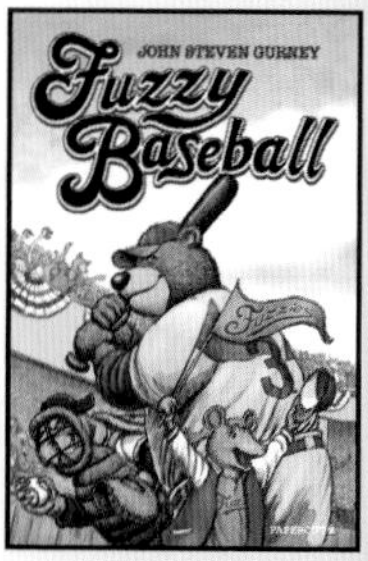
JOHN STEVEN GURNEY
Fuzzy Baseball
FUZZY BASEBALL

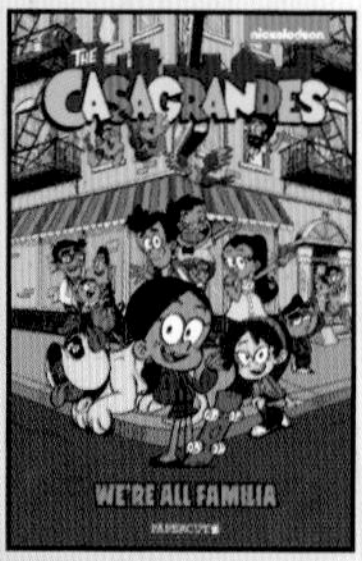
THE CASAGRANDES
WE'RE ALL FAMILIA
THE CASAGRANDES

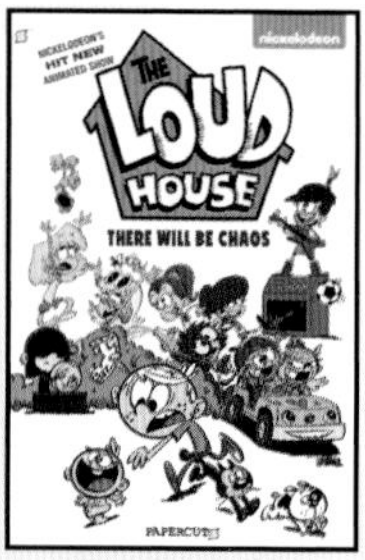
THE LOUD HOUSE
THERE WILL BE CHAOS
THE LOUD HOUSE

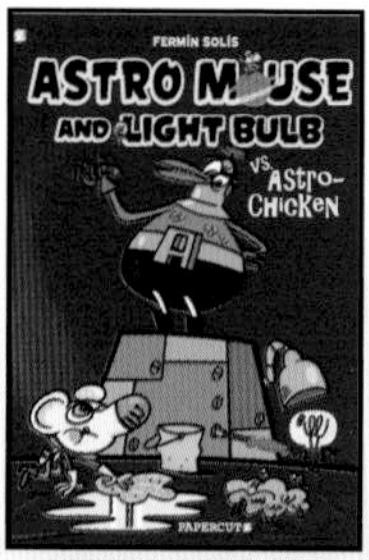
FERMÍN SOLÍS
ASTRO MOUSE AND LIGHT BULB
VS Astro-Chicken
ASTRO MOUSE AND LIGHT BULB

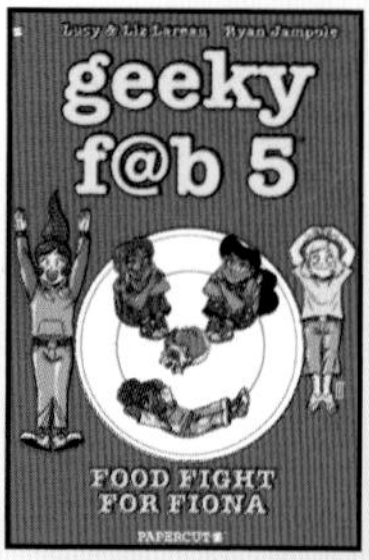
geeky f@b 5
FOOD FIGHT FOR FIONA
GEEKY F@B 5

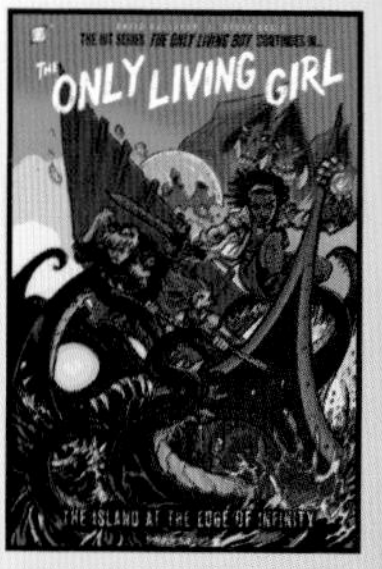
THE ONLY LIVING GIRL
THE ISLAND AT THE EDGE OF INFINITY
THE ONLY LIVING GIRL

papercutz.com

Also available where ebooks are sold.

THE LOUD HOUSE

#17 "SIBLING RIVALRY"

#17 "SIBLING RIVALRY"

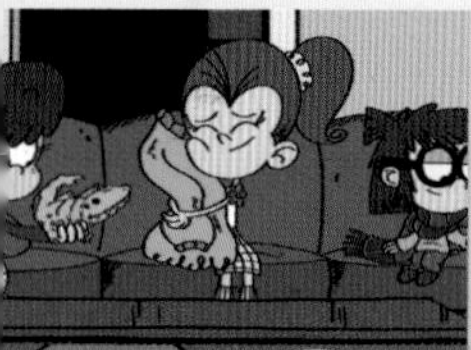

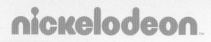

"A COZY COMPULSION"
Erik Steinman — Writer
Amanda Lioi — Artist, Colorist
Wilson Ramos Jr. — Letterer

"HAZARDOUS CONDITIONS"
Derek Fridolfs — Writer
Marc Stone — Artist
Laurie E. Smith — Colorist
Wilson Ramos Jr. — Letterer

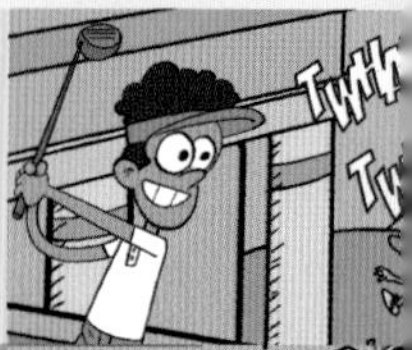

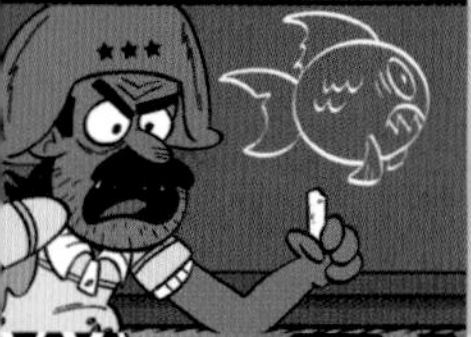

"FISH OUT OF WATER"
Derek Fridolfs — Writer
Lex Hobson— Artist, Colorist
Wilson Ramos Jr. — Letterer

"FAMILY A CALLING"
Kacey Huang-Wooley — Writer
Lex Hobson — Artist, Colorist
Wilson Ramos Jr. — Letterer

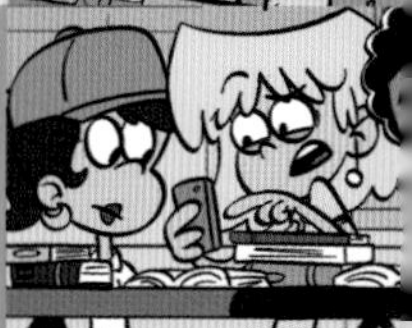

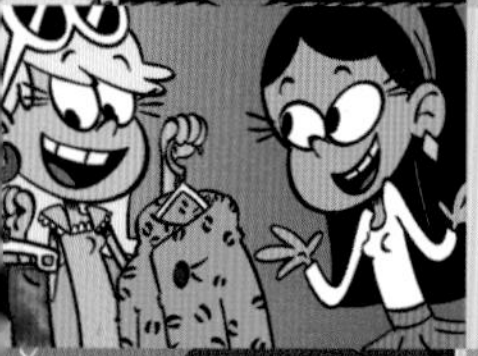

"TRENDFRETTER"
Erik Steinman — Writer
Lex Hobson — Artist, Colorist
Wilson Ramos Jr. — Letterer

"A NOT SO CLOSE ENCOUNTER'"
Kara and Amanda Fein — Writers
Melissa Kleynowski — Artist
Laurie E. Smith — Colorist
Wilson Ramos Jr. — Letterer

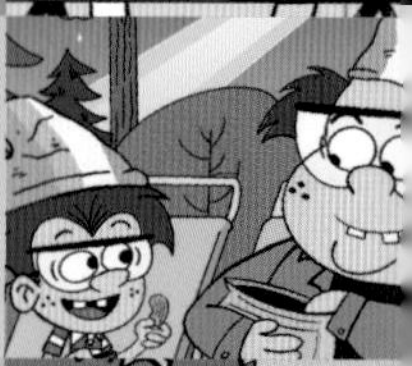

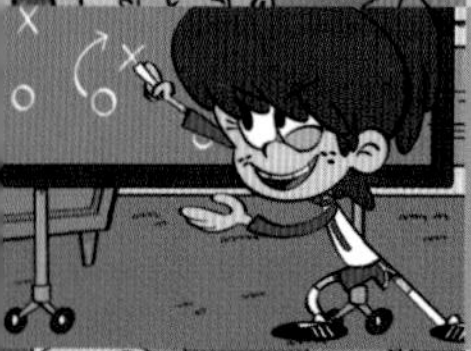

"LYNN IT TO WIN IT"
Derek Fridolfs — Writer
Olivia Walden — Artist
Lex Hobson — Colorist
Wilson Ramos Jr. — Letterer

"A PETTY PLAYDATE"
Kacey Huang-Wooley — Writer
Erin Hyde — Artist, Colorist
Wilson Ramos Jr. — Letterer

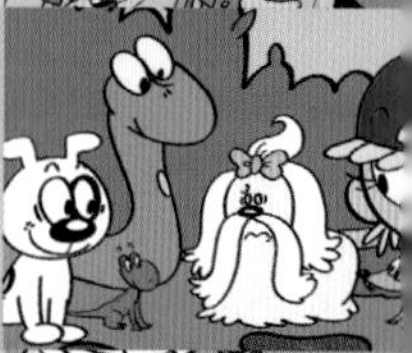

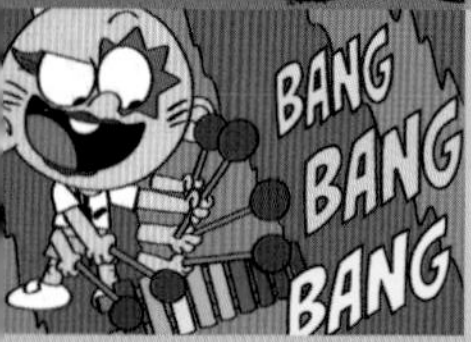
BANG
BANG
BANG

"ROCK N' ROLE MODEL"
Amanda Lioi — Writer, Artist, Colorist
Wilson Ramos Jr. — Letterer

MELISSA KLEYNOWSKI — Cover Artist
PETER BERTUCCI — Cover Colorist

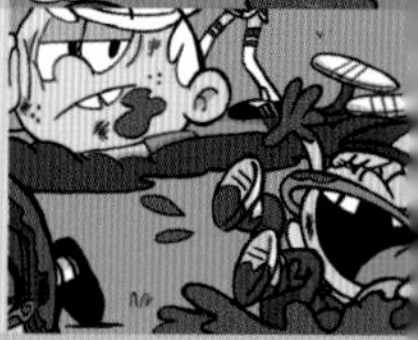

JAYJAY JACKSON — Design
KRISTEN G. SMITH, DANA CLUVERIUS, MOLLIE FREILICH, NEIL WADE, MIGUEL PUGA,
LALO ALCARAZ, JOAN HILTY, KRISTEN YU-UM, EMILIE CRUZ, and ARTHUR "DJ" DESIN— Special Thanks
KARLO ANTUNES — Editor
STEPHANIE BROOKS — Assistant Managing Editor
JEFF WHITMAN — Comics Editor/Nickelodeon
MICOL HIATT — Comics Designer/Nickelodeon
JIM SALICRUP
Editor-in-Chief

ISBN: 978-1-5458-0979-2 paperback edition
ISBN: 978-1-5458-0977-8 hardcover edition

www.papercutz.com

Papercutz books may be purchased for business or promotional use. For information on bulk purchases please contact Macmillan Corporate and Premium Sales Department at (800) 221-7945 x5442.

Printed in China
November 2022

Distributed by Macmillan
First Printing

MEET THE LOUD FAMILY *and friends!*

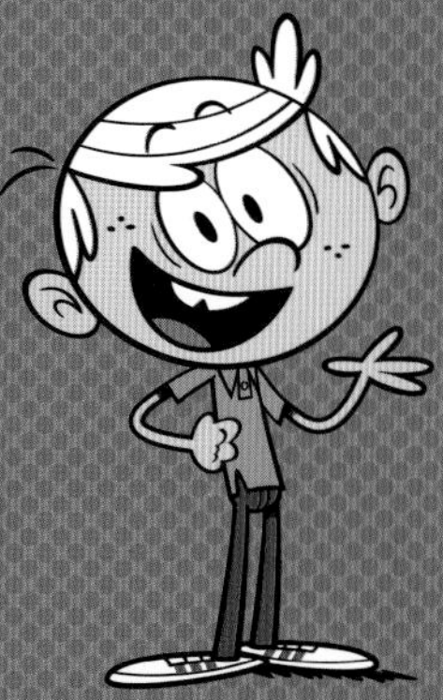

LINCOLN LOUD
THE MIDDLE CHILD

Lincoln is the middle child, with five older sisters and five younger sisters. He has learned that surviving the Loud household means staying a step ahead. As the "man with a plan," he's always coming up with a way to get what he wants or deal with a problem, even if things inevitably go wrong. But don't worry, Lincoln's got a backup plan for that, too. He loves comicbooks, video games, magic, fantasy and science fiction stories – all of which you might find him enjoying in his underwear. His favorite characters include secret agent David Steele (think James Bond), superhero Ace Savvy (think Superman with a knack for playing-card puns) and video game protagonist Muscle Fish.
He and his best friend Clyde make up the dynamic duo, Clincoln McCloud! They, along with his best friends (collectively known as "the Action News Team" because of the reporting they do for the school news program), always stick together – it's the best way to survive middle school.

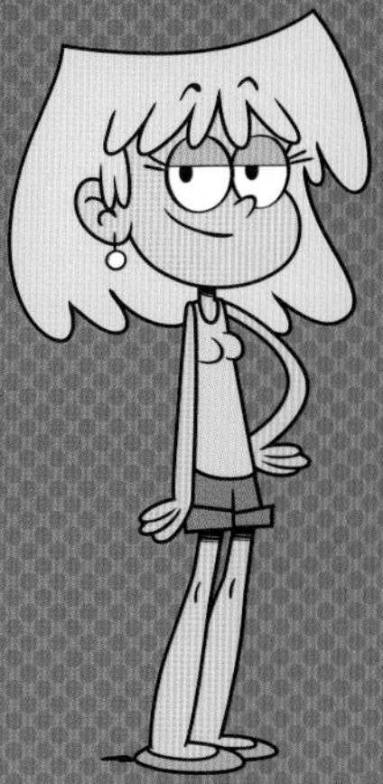

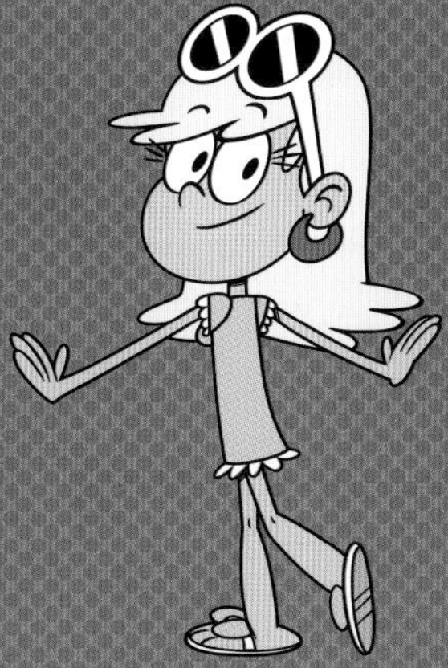

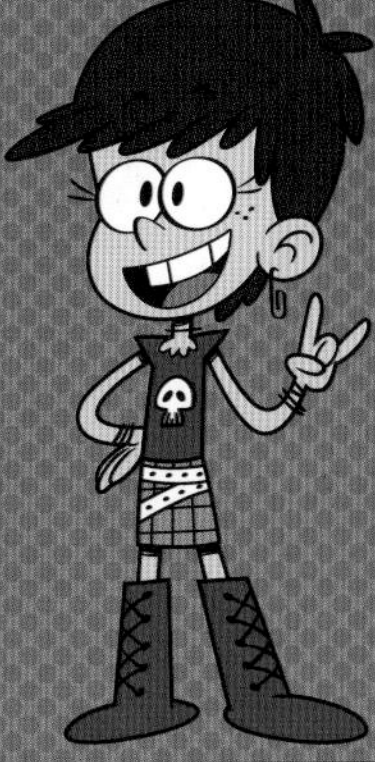

LORI LOUD
THE OLDEST

Lori's the first-born child of the Loud clan, and therefore sees herself as the boss of all her siblings. She feels she's paved the way for them and deserves extra respect. Her signature traits are rolling her eyes, texting her boyfriend Bobby (AKA "Boo-Boo Bear"), and literally saying "literally" all the time. Because she's the oldest and most experienced sibling, Lori can be a great ally, so it pays to stay on her good side, especially since she can drive.
Lori has begun attending Fairway University, a prestigious golf college, and is one of the youngest players to make the school's golf team. Even though she's moved away from home, she's always in touch with her siblings. Even at college, Lori is always part of the Loud family shenanigans.

LENI LOUD
THE FASHIONISTA

Leni spends most of her time designing outfits, accessorizing, and shopping at the mall – which makes her the perfect sales employee at Reininger's department store. Her people-pleasing nature, natural leadership abilities, and fashion instincts keep customers coming back! Leni is supported by her best friends and co-workers, Miguel and Fiona (and sometimes Tanya the mannequin). And now she has the added support of her new boyfriend, Gavin, who works in the mall food court.
Back at the house, she always falls for Luan's pranks, and sometimes walks into walls when she's talking (she's not great at doing two things at once). But what Leni lacks in smarts, she makes up for in heart. She's the sweetest Loud around!

LUNA LOUD
THE ROCK STAR

Luna is loud, boisterous and freewheeling, and her energy is always cranked to 11. On the off-chance she doesn't have her guitar with her, everything can and will be turned into a musical instrument. You can always count on Luna to help out, and she'll do most anything you ask, as long as you're okay with her supplying a rocking musical accompaniment.
When she's not jamming, Luna is most likely hanging out with her girlfriend, Sam, or playing with their band, The Moon Goats. The two might even be found babysitting the McBride's cats – it turns out Sam's a natural cat whisperer!

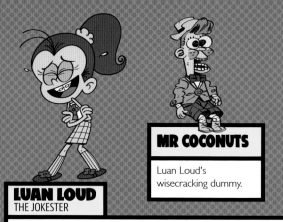

MR COCONUTS

Luan Loud's wisecracking dummy.

LUAN LOUD
THE JOKESTER

Luan is a standup comedienne who provides a nonstop barrage of silly puns. She's big on prop comedy – squirting flowers and whoopee cushions – so you have to be on your toes whenever she's around. She loves to pull pranks – April Fool's Day is her favorite day (and the rest of the Louds' least favorite). Luan is also a really good ventriloquist – she is often found doing bits with her dummy, Mr. Coconuts (but don't let him hear you calling him a "dummy"). At school, Luan and her boyfriend, Benny, are usually writing and performing in the high school's theatrical productions – under the somewhat melodramatic supervision of their drama teacher, Mrs. Bernardo. Luan has also reached new heights while playing Dairyland character Heidi Heifer during the theme park's season.

LYNN LOUD
THE ATHLETE

Lynn is athletic, full of energy, and always looking for a challenge or competition. She can turn anything into a sport. Putting away eggs? Jump shot! Score! Cleaning up the eggs? Slap shot! Score! Despite her competitive nature, Lynn always tries to have a good time with her family... and her teammates and best friends Paula and Margo. At school, she takes her duties as hall monitor seriously and doesn't tolerate any slackers... but she also shows a lot of heart when looking after Lincoln in his first year at middle school. One super fun fact about Lynn: her name is really Lynn Jr. (L.J.), because she's named after Dad!

LUCY LOUD
THE EMO

Lucy can always be counted on to give the morbid point of view in any given situation. She is obsessed with all things spooky and dark – funerals, vampires, séances... you get the idea. Lucy has a way of mysteriously appearing out of nowhere, and try as they might, her siblings never get used to this. She loves the character of Edwin from the TV show "Vampires of Melancholia," and has a homemade bust of him hidden in her closet.

Lucy spends most of her time with her friends in the Morticians Club, of which she is a co-president. Together, the club speaks to spirits, attends casket conventions, and rides around in a hearse (well, technically it's just a station wagon painted black). Their motto is "Keep Calm and Embalm."

LOLA LOUD
THE BEAUTY QUEEN

Lola is a pageant powerhouse whose interests include glitter, photo shoots, and her own beautiful, beautiful face. But don't let her cute, gap-toothed smile fool you; underneath all the sugar and spice lurks a Machiavellian mastermind. Whatever Lola wants, Lola gets – or else. She's the eyes and ears of the household and never resists an opportunity to tattle on troublemakers. But if you stay on Lola's good side, you've got yourself a fierce ally – and a credit line to the first national bank of Lola. She might even let you drive her around in her pink jeep while she practices her pageant wave.

BITEY

LANA LOUD
THE TOMBOY

Lana is the rough-and-tumble sparkplug counterpart to her twin sister, Lola. She's all about animals, mud pies, and muffler repairs. She's the resident Ms. Fix-it and animal whisperer, and is always ready to lend a hand – the dirtier the job, the better. Need your toilet unclogged? Snake trained? Back-zit popped? Lana's your gal. All she asks in return is a handful of kibble (she often sneaks it from the dog bowl anyway) or anything you can fish out of a nearby garbage can. She's proud of who she is, and her big heart definitely overpowers her pungent dumpster smell. Needless to say, while the twins love each other deep down, they've been known to get into some pretty epic brawls, mud and sequins flying. But when they join forces (like the time they pretended to be each other for their own personal gain), the rest of the Louds had better look out.

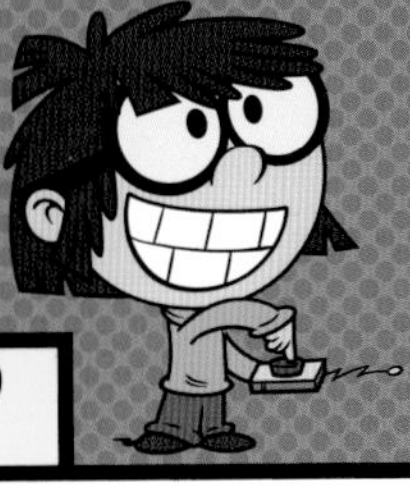

LISA LOUD
THE GENIUS

Lisa is smarter than the rest of her siblings combined, which would still be big news even if she wasn't only four years old. Lisa spends most of her time working in her bedroom lab (the family has gotten used to the explosions), and says her research leaves little time for frivolous pursuits like "playing" or "human interaction." Despite this, she can still find time to unwind with a little bit of West coast rap. She has a collection of robot companions that she's created over the years, but these days relies mostly on Todd, her newest (and sassiest) mechanical friend. Together they've traveled back in time, launched themselves into outer space, and enjoyed many hours watching Todd's favorite TV show, "Robot Dance Party." At school (where Lisa is smarter than her teacher), she is learning to enjoy social interaction with her friend Darcy, but will forego nap time to work on all the top secret projects she's got going on with the Norwegian government.

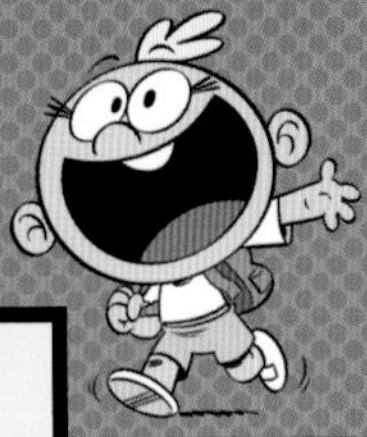

LILY LOUD
THE BABY

Lily's the baby of the family, but she's growing up fast. She's a toddler now and can speak full sentences– well, sometimes. As an infant she was already mischievous, but now she's upped her game. Her most important goal – other than tricking the family into taking her for ice cream – is to impress the other pre-school kids at show and tell. No matter what, though, she still brings a smile to everyone's faces, and the family loves her unconditionally.

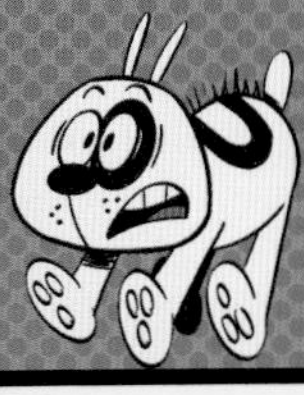

CHARLES

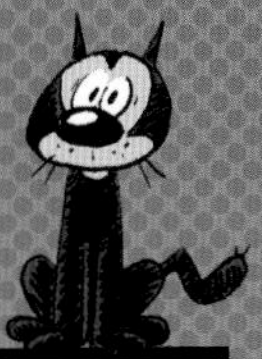

CLIFF

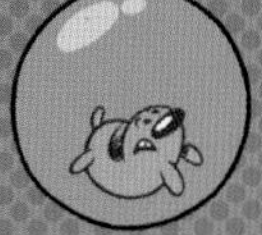

GEO

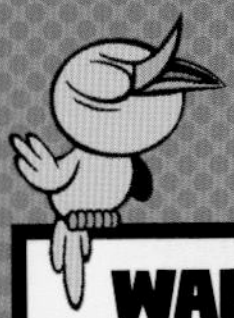

WALT

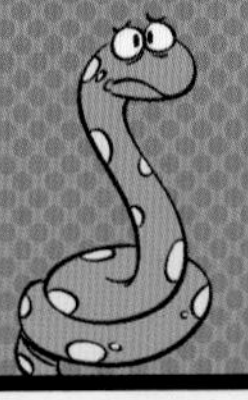

EL DIABLO

RITA LOUD

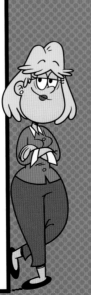

Mother to the eleven Loud kids, Mom Rita wears many different hats. She's a chauffeur, homework-checker and barf cleaner-upper all rolled into one. Mom is organized and keeps the family running like a well-oiled machine. She's always there for her kids and ready to jump into action during a crisis, whether it's a fight between the twins or finding Leni's missing shoe. When she's not chasing the kids, she's a columnist for the Royal Woods Gazette. As a skilled writer, she's able to connect with her readers as a mom simply trying to do her best. She also loves taking on house projects and is very handy with tools (guess that's where Lana gets it from). Between writing her novel, working on her column, and being a mom, her days are always hectic - but she wouldn't have it any other way.

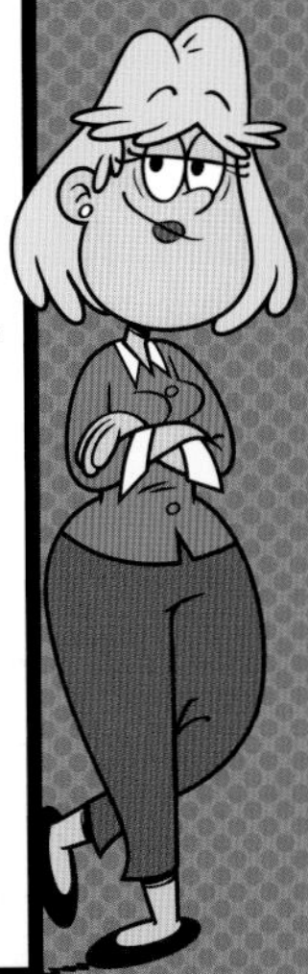

LYNN LOUD SR.

Dad (Lynn Loud Sr.) is a fun-loving, upbeat chef and owner of Lynn's Table – a family style restaurant that specializes in serving delicious but outrageously named meals like Lynn-sagna and Lynn-ger chicken. A sentimental kid-at-heart, he's not above taking part in the kids' zany schemes but is more well known for the emotions he wears on his sleeves: his sobbing – both for joy and sadness – is legendary. In addition to cooking, Dad loves his van (affectionately named Vanzilla), British culture, and making puns with any of the kids not already rolling their eyes. Most of all, Dad loves rocking out with his best friend and head waiter, Kotaro. They're part of a cowbell-focused band with some other dads in Royal Woods; hence their band name: The Doo-Dads.

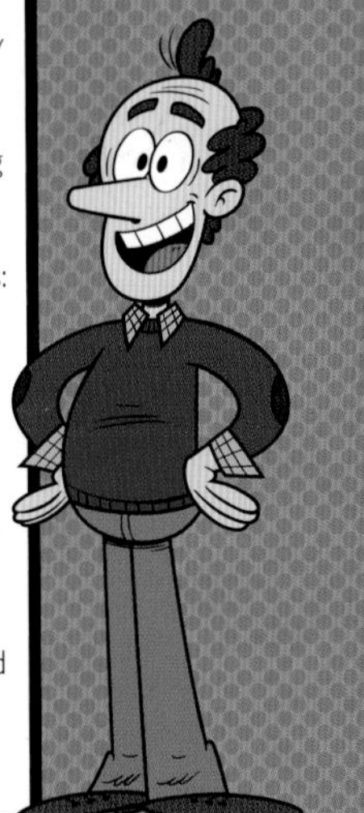

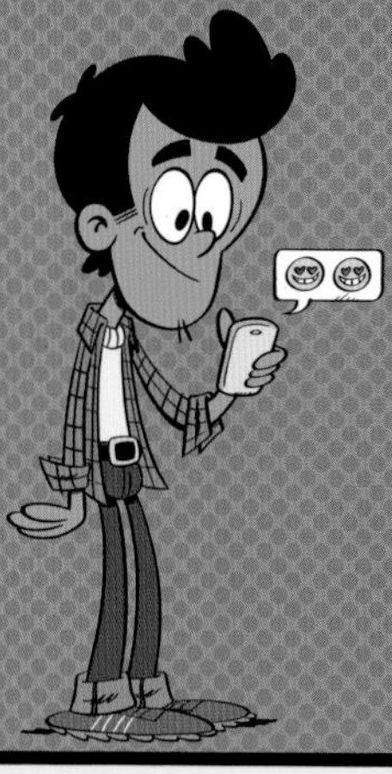

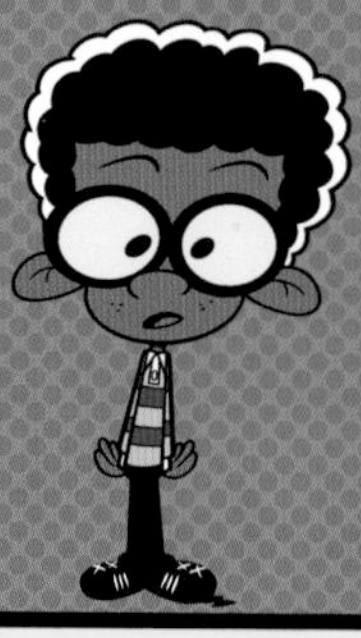

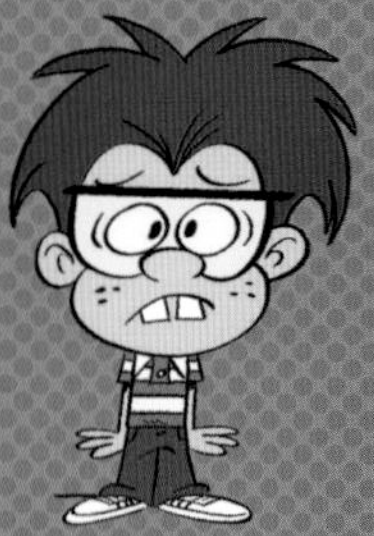

BOBBY SANTIAGO

Bobby is Ronnie Anne's big bro. He's a student and one of the hardest workers in the city. He loves his family and loves working at the *mercado*. As his *abuelo's* right hand man, Bobby can't wait to take over the family business one day. He's a big kid at heart, and his clumsiness gets him into some sticky situations at work, like locking himself in the freezer. *Mercado* mishaps aside, everyone in the neighborhood loves to come to the store and talk to Bobby.

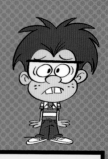

CLYDE McBRIDE

Clyde is Lincoln's best friend in the whole world… so it probably goes without saying that he's also Lincoln's partner in crime. Clyde is always willing to go along with Lincoln's crazy schemes, even if he sees the flaws in them up-front or if they sometimes give him anxiety tummy aches. Lincoln and Clyde are two peas in a pod and share pretty much all of the same tastes in movies, comics, TV shows, toys—you name it. Clyde knows exactly who he is and is not afraid to show it! As an only child, Clyde envies Lincoln—how cool would it be to always have siblings around to talk to? But since Clyde spends so much time at the Loud house, he's almost an honorary sibling anyway. Clyde is a little neurotic, but that's probably because he's the son of helicopter dads, Howard and Harold. They are VERY over-protective and VERY involved in his life. Clyde isn't spoiled, he's just extremely well-cared for. But he's slowly learning to stand on his own two feet and his dads are starting to see how well he can take care of himself.

ZACH GURDLE

Lincoln's pal Zach is a self- admitted nerd who's obsessed with aliens and conspiracy theories. (He's just following in the footsteps of his alien hunting parents.) Zach lives between a freeway and a circus, so the chaos of the Loud House doesn't faze him. To Zach, everything is a mystery to be solved or coverup to be exposed. His best friend in the gang is Rusty, with whom he occasionally butts heads. But deep down, it's all love.

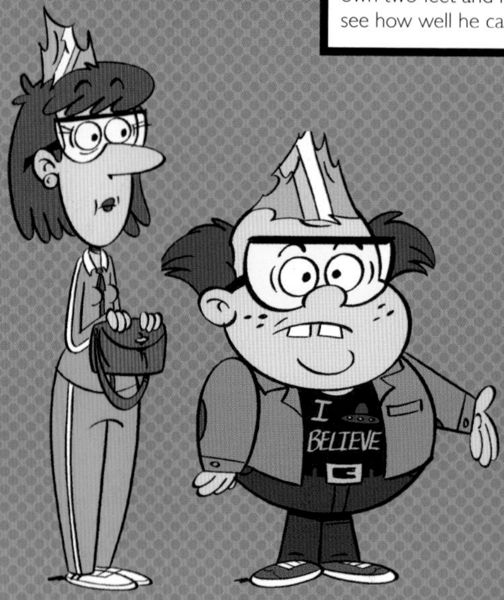
I BELIEVE

MR. AND MRS. GURDLE

The parents to one of Lincoln's best friends, Zach, the Gurdles are just as eccentric as their son. The Gurdles love conspiracy theories and all things outside the realm of "normal." They take their beliefs to such extremes that they walk around with homemade foil antennas on their heads at all times, in hopes of picking up alien signals. Despite their nerdy ways, they are loving parents who take a more unconventional approach to parenting than most.

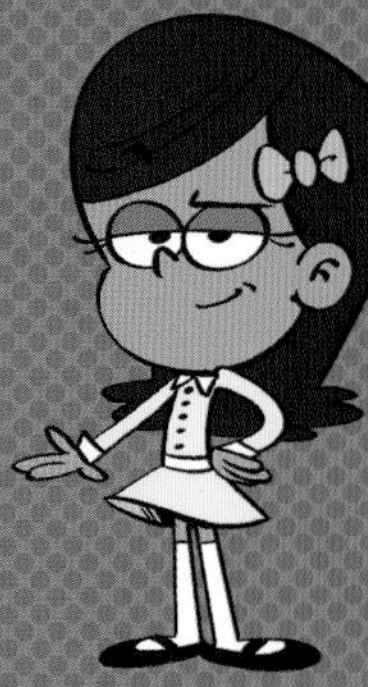

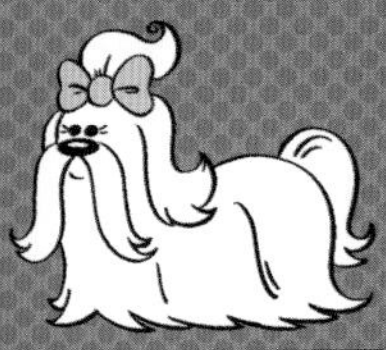

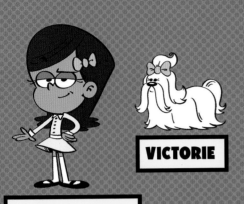

VICTORIE

LACEY ST. CLAIR

Lacey St. Clair is Lana's snobby, aristocratic classmate who looks down on the Loud Family dog, Charles, with haughty judgment. As far as Lacey's concerned, her purebred long-haired Maltese, Victorie, is the epitome of true doggy sophistication—as attested by her many Royal Woods Dog show trophies.

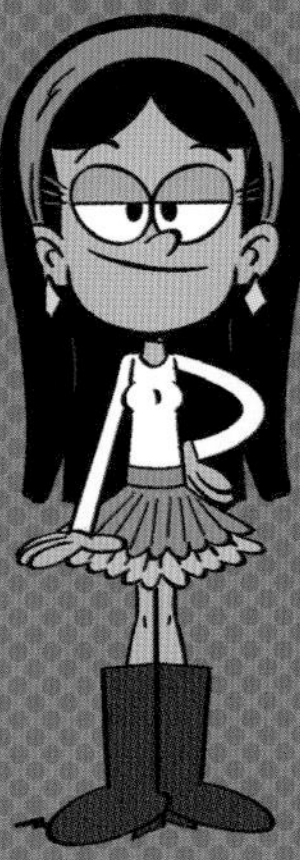

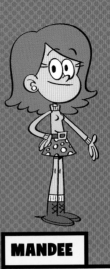

JACKIE

Goes to school with Leni and Mandee. She loves fashion, using hip teen slang, and never misses an issue of 16 and a half magazine.

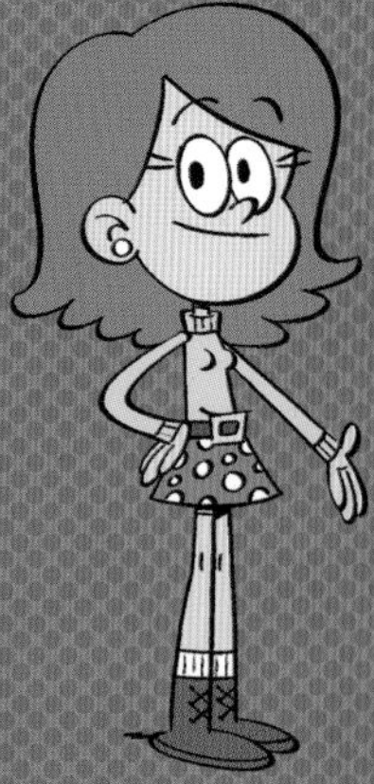

MANDEE

Goes to school with Leni and Jackie. She loves pumpkin spice lattes, popup sales at the mall, and air kisses.

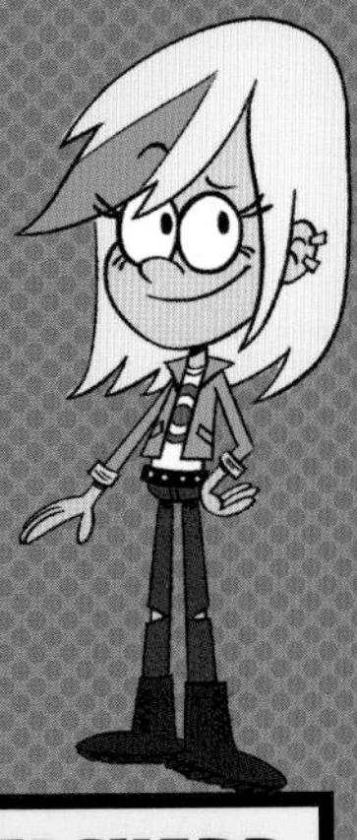

SAM SHARP

Sam is Luna's girlfriend and a member of the Moon Goats. She's sweet and kind, and is able to keep her feet on the ground even as she and Luna dream of a famous future. She helps keep Luna grounded, too, always turning a negative (the fact they may not have much in common at first) into a positive (it gives them so many new things to do together).

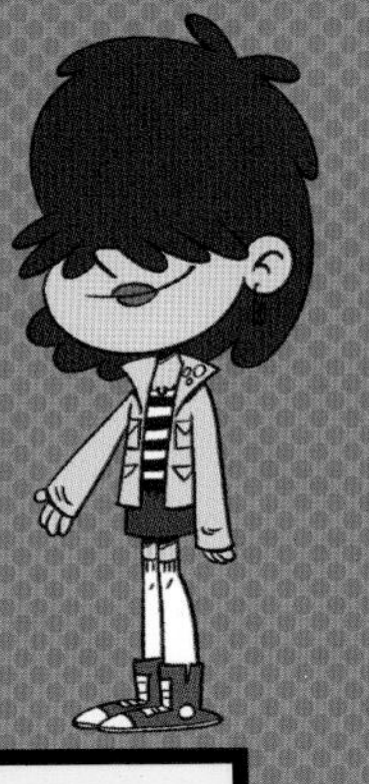

MAZZY

Mazzy is Luna's classmate at Royal Woods High School, and the drummer in her band, The Moon Goats. Mazzy has a cool rocker fashion vibe, a witty, dry sense of humor, and a pet tarantula.

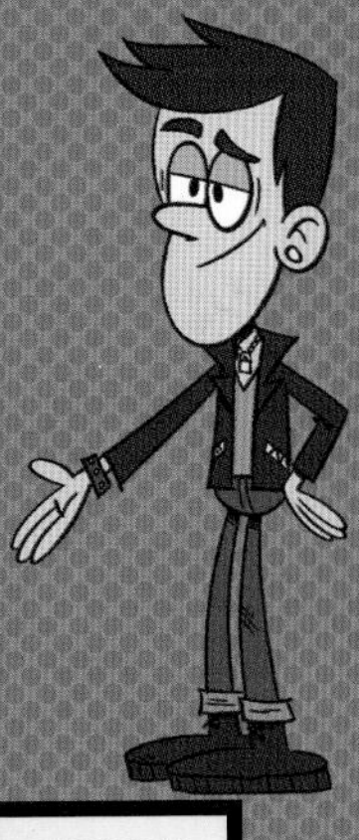

SULLY

Sully is also Luna's classmate and a member of The Moon Goats. He's known for his chill, lowkey attitude – nothing rattles him. Sometimes, though, it takes him a moment or two to catch on to what's happening around him.

RUSTY SPOKES

Lincoln's friend Rusty is a self-proclaimed ladies' man who's always the first to dish out girl advice— even though he's never been on an actual date. No one has more confidence than Rusty, even if that confidence is often completely misguided. Rusty's a looker – at least in his own eyes – and is always working hard to protect his face (what he calls his "moneymaker"). Rusty is always sharing advice from his experienced but equally delusional cousin, Derek. No matter what the situation, it seems like Derek's been there before and lived to tell about it. Rusty's dad, Rodney, owns a clothing store called "Duds for Dudes," so he can always hook the gang up with some dapper duds—just as long as no one gets anything dirty.

LIAM HUNNICUTT

Lincoln's friend Liam is an enthusiastic, sweet-natured farm boy full of down-home wisdom. He loves hanging out with his Mee Maw, wrestling his prize pig Virginia, and sharing his farm-to-table produce with the rest of the gang. No matter the situation, Liam faces it with optimism.

STELLA ZHAU

Lincoln's pal Stella is a tech genius, always building new devices – usually from parts she's salvaged from old devices. She loves to take things apart just to see how they work. Her smarts help keep the gang focused and on track, especially when they're chasing a news story. Stella will happily take charge of a situation – she's helped solve many a school mystery and even improved the gang's shield formation defense in dodgeball.

TODD BOT

While Todd is just one of the many robots Lisa's built, he's definitely her favorite (ssshh, don't tell the others!). He's outspoken and opinionated, and sometimes a little too sassy for Lisa (which is why she installed a button to dial down the sassiness). Still, she relies on him for everything, from coordinating scientific presentations worldwide, to building rockets and time travel devices, to providing a funky beat she can rap to. Todd is a loyal companion to Lisa - except, you know, when someone accidentally flips his "villain" switch, and then he just wants to destroy Royal Woods (but this rarely happens so it's all good).

MARISA

Marisa is Lori's supportive and optimistic college roommate at Fairway University. With the help of her inspirational golf quote calendar, she always has the solution to Lori's problems… golf-related or not.

"A COZY COMPULSION"

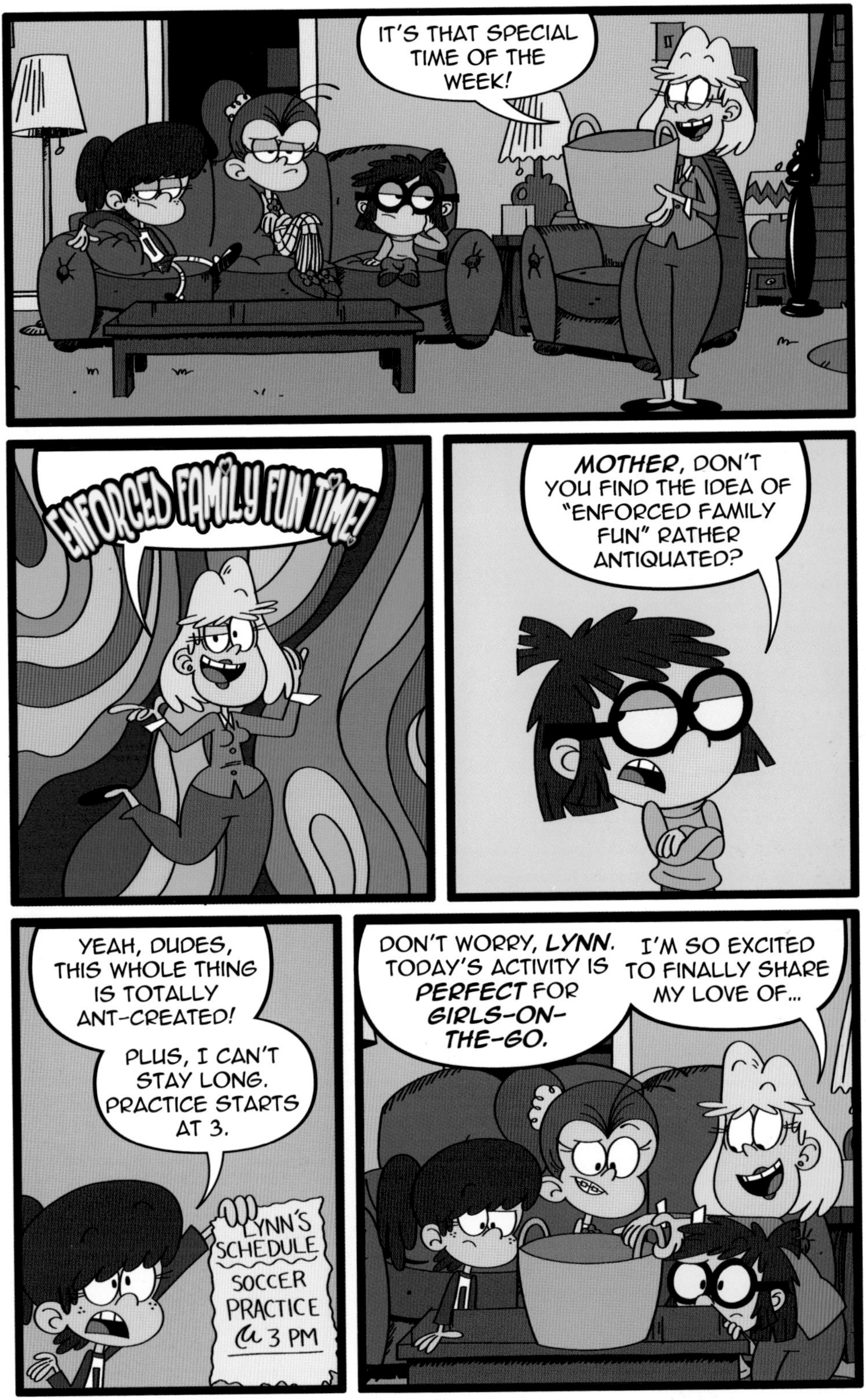

IT'S THAT SPECIAL TIME OF THE WEEK!
ENFORCED FAMILY FUN TIME!
MOTHER, DON'T YOU FIND THE IDEA OF "ENFORCED FAMILY FUN" RATHER ANTIQUATED?
YEAH, DUDES, THIS WHOLE THING IS TOTALLY ANT-CREATED!
PLUS, I CAN'T STAY LONG. PRACTICE STARTS AT 3.
LYNN'S SCHEDULE
SOCCER PRACTICE @ 3 PM
DON'T WORRY, LYNN. TODAY'S ACTIVITY IS PERFECT FOR GIRLS-ON-THE-GO.
I'M SO EXCITED TO FINALLY SHARE MY LOVE OF...

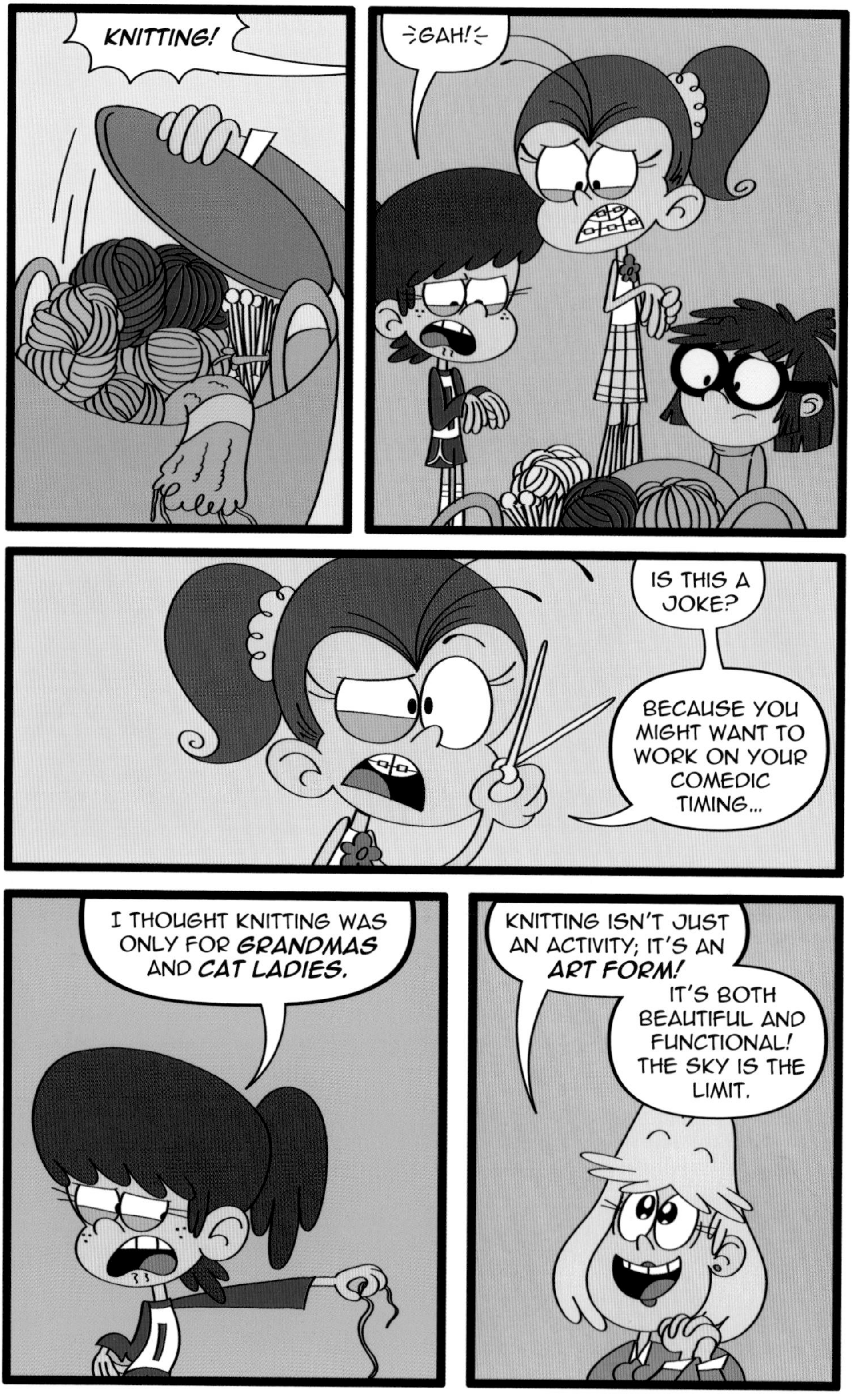
KNITTING!
GAH!
IS THIS A JOKE?
BECAUSE YOU MIGHT WANT TO WORK ON YOUR COMEDIC TIMING...
I THOUGHT KNITTING WAS ONLY FOR GRANDMAS AND CAT LADIES.
KNITTING ISN'T JUST AN ACTIVITY; IT'S AN ART FORM!
IT'S BOTH BEAUTIFUL AND FUNCTIONAL! THE SKY IS THE LIMIT.

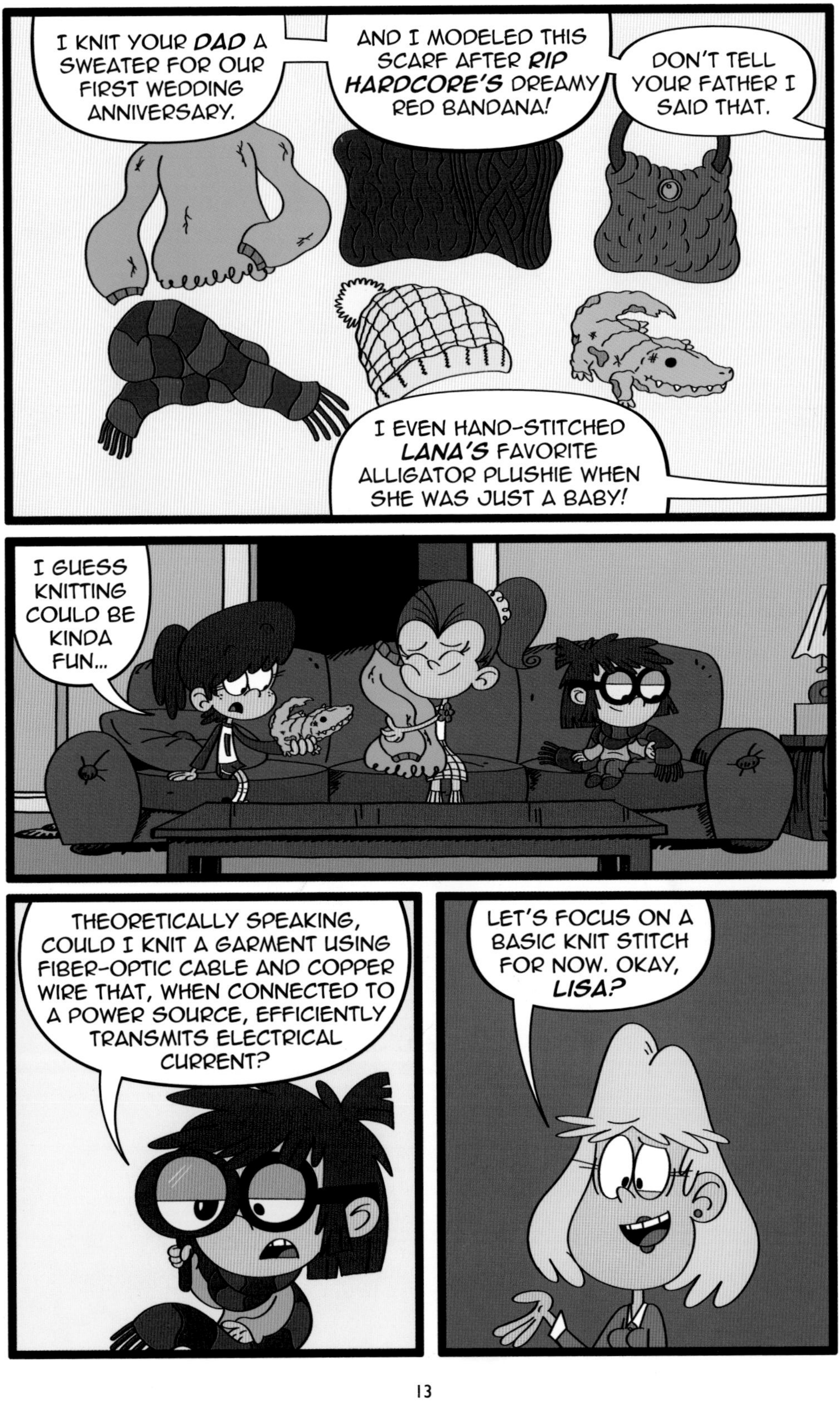
I KNIT YOUR DAD A SWEATER FOR OUR FIRST WEDDING ANNIVERSARY.
AND I MODELED THIS SCARF AFTER RIP HARDCORE'S DREAMY RED BANDANA!
DON'T TELL YOUR FATHER I SAID THAT.
I EVEN HAND-STITCHED LANA'S FAVORITE ALLIGATOR PLUSHIE WHEN SHE WAS JUST A BABY!
I GUESS KNITTING COULD BE KINDA FUN...
THEORETICALLY SPEAKING, COULD I KNIT A GARMENT USING FIBER-OPTIC CABLE AND COPPER WIRE THAT, WHEN CONNECTED TO A POWER SOURCE, EFFICIENTLY TRANSMITS ELECTRICAL CURRENT?
LET'S FOCUS ON A BASIC KNIT STITCH FOR NOW. OKAY, LISA?

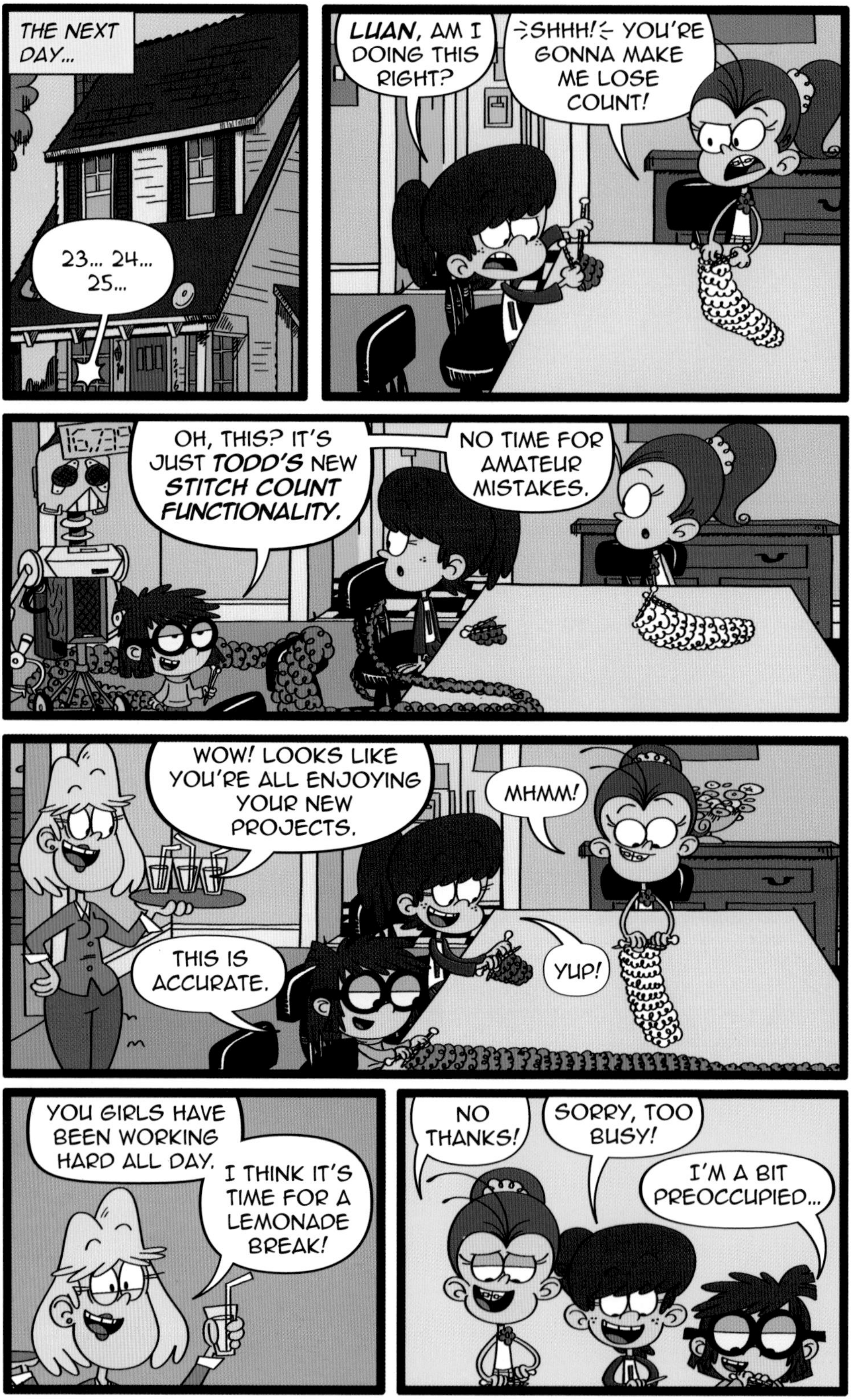
THE NEXT DAY...
23... 24... 25...
LUAN, AM I DOING THIS RIGHT?
SHHH! YOU'RE GONNA MAKE ME LOSE COUNT!
16,739
OH, THIS? IT'S JUST TODD'S NEW STITCH COUNT FUNCTIONALITY.
NO TIME FOR AMATEUR MISTAKES.
WOW! LOOKS LIKE YOU'RE ALL ENJOYING YOUR NEW PROJECTS.
MHMM!
THIS IS ACCURATE.
YUP!
YOU GIRLS HAVE BEEN WORKING HARD ALL DAY.
I THINK IT'S TIME FOR A LEMONADE BREAK!
NO THANKS!
SORRY, TOO BUSY!
I'M A BIT PREOCCUPIED...

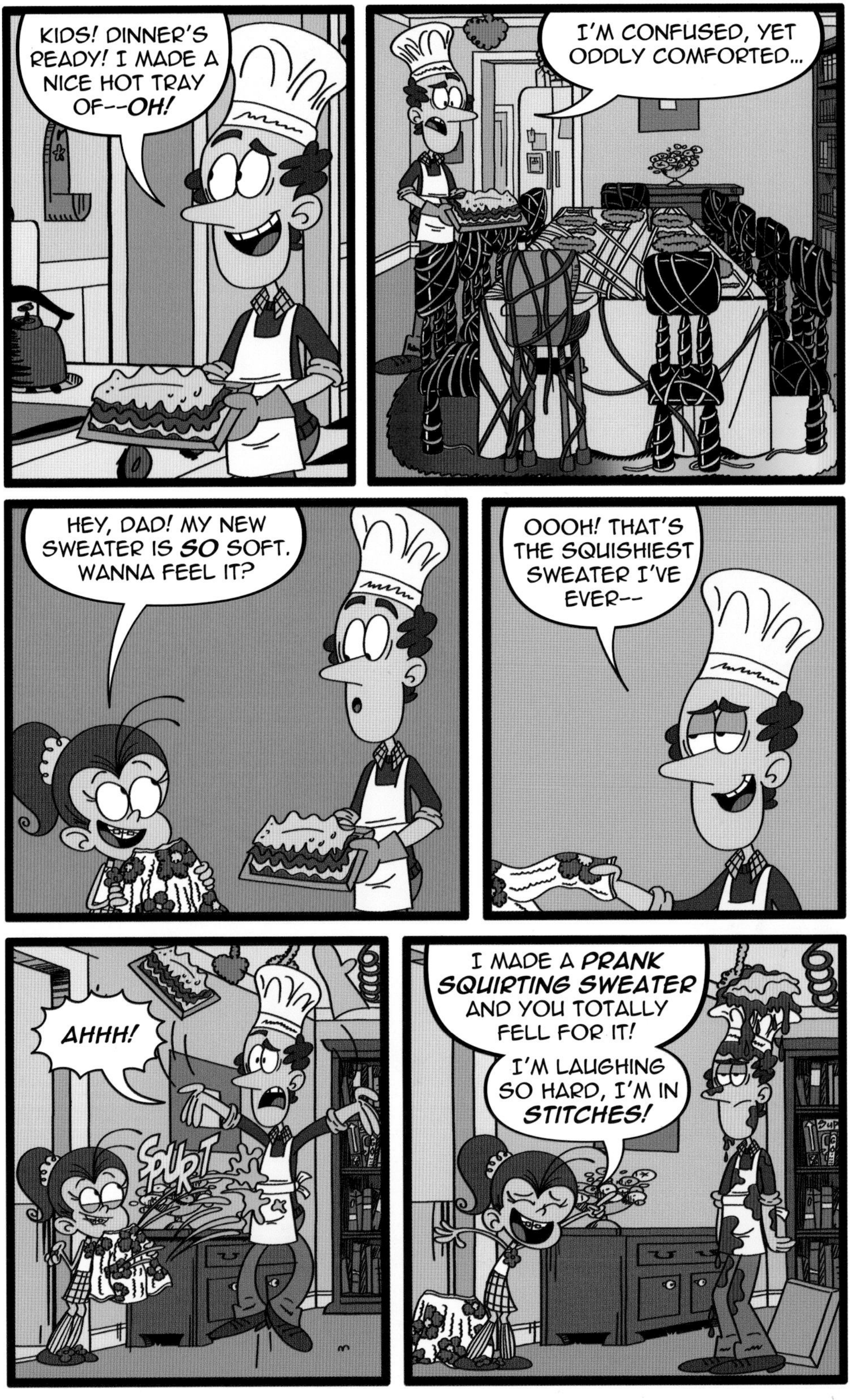
KIDS! DINNER'S READY! I MADE A NICE HOT TRAY OF--OH!
I'M CONFUSED, YET ODDLY COMFORTED...
HEY, DAD! MY NEW SWEATER IS SO SOFT. WANNA FEEL IT?
OOOH! THAT'S THE SQUISHIEST SWEATER I'VE EVER--
AHHH!
SPURT
I MADE A PRANK SQUIRTING SWEATER AND YOU TOTALLY FELL FOR IT!
I'M LAUGHING SO HARD, I'M IN STITCHES!

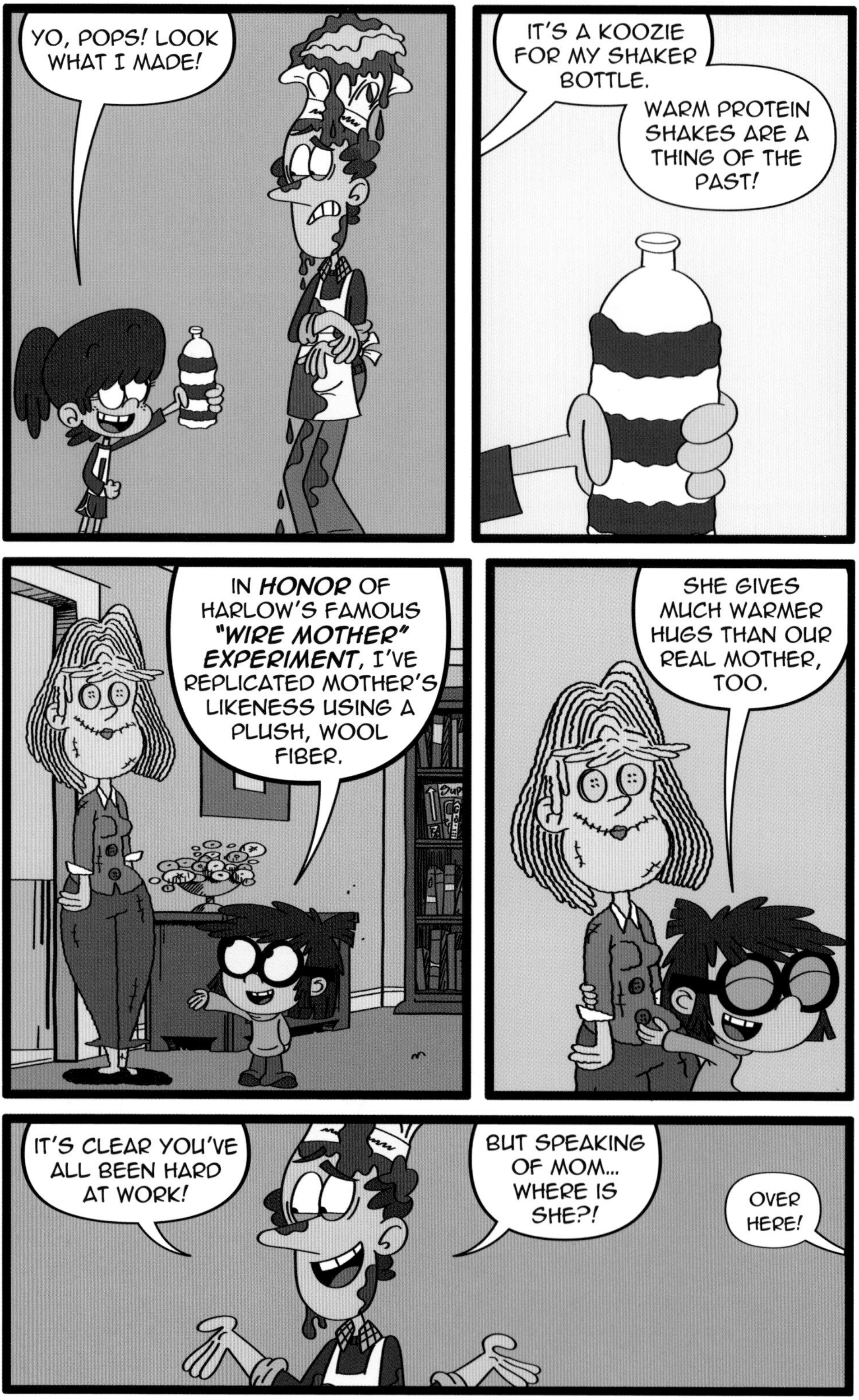
YO, POPS! LOOK WHAT I MADE!
IT'S A KOOZIE FOR MY SHAKER BOTTLE.
WARM PROTEIN SHAKES ARE A THING OF THE PAST!
IN **HONOR** OF HARLOW'S FAMOUS ***"WIRE MOTHER" EXPERIMENT***, I'VE REPLICATED MOTHER'S LIKENESS USING A PLUSH, WOOL FIBER.
SHE GIVES MUCH WARMER HUGS THAN OUR REAL MOTHER, TOO.
IT'S CLEAR YOU'VE ALL BEEN HARD AT WORK!
BUT SPEAKING OF MOM... WHERE IS SHE?!
OVER HERE!

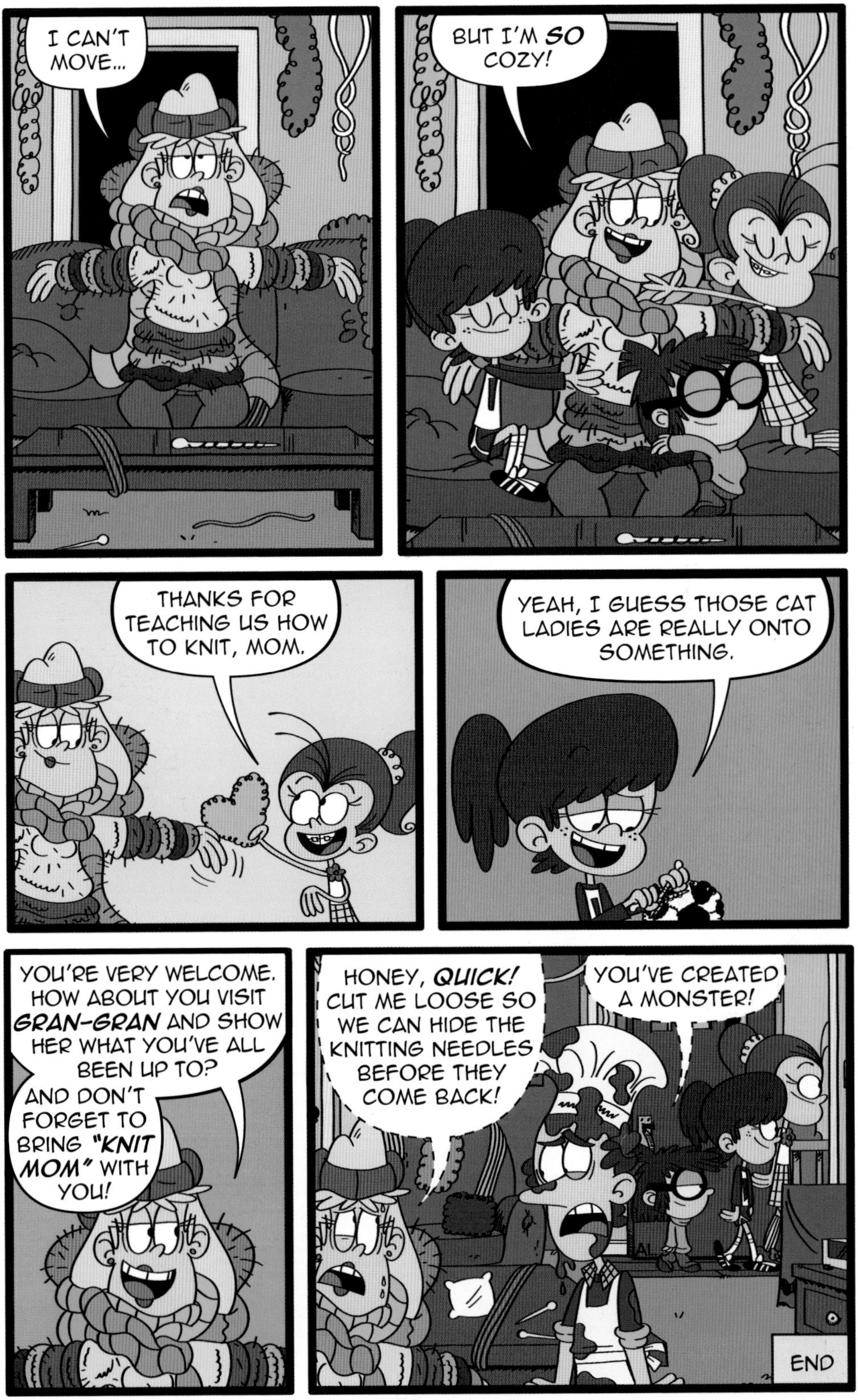
I CAN'T MOVE...
BUT I'M SO COZY!
THANKS FOR TEACHING US HOW TO KNIT, MOM.
YEAH, I GUESS THOSE CAT LADIES ARE REALLY ONTO SOMETHING.
YOU'RE VERY WELCOME. HOW ABOUT YOU VISIT GRAN-GRAN AND SHOW HER WHAT YOU'VE ALL BEEN UP TO?
AND DON'T FORGET TO BRING "KNIT MOM" WITH YOU!
HONEY, QUICK! CUT ME LOOSE SO WE CAN HIDE THE KNITTING NEEDLES BEFORE THEY COME BACK!
YOU'VE CREATED A MONSTER!
END

"FISH OUT OF WATER"

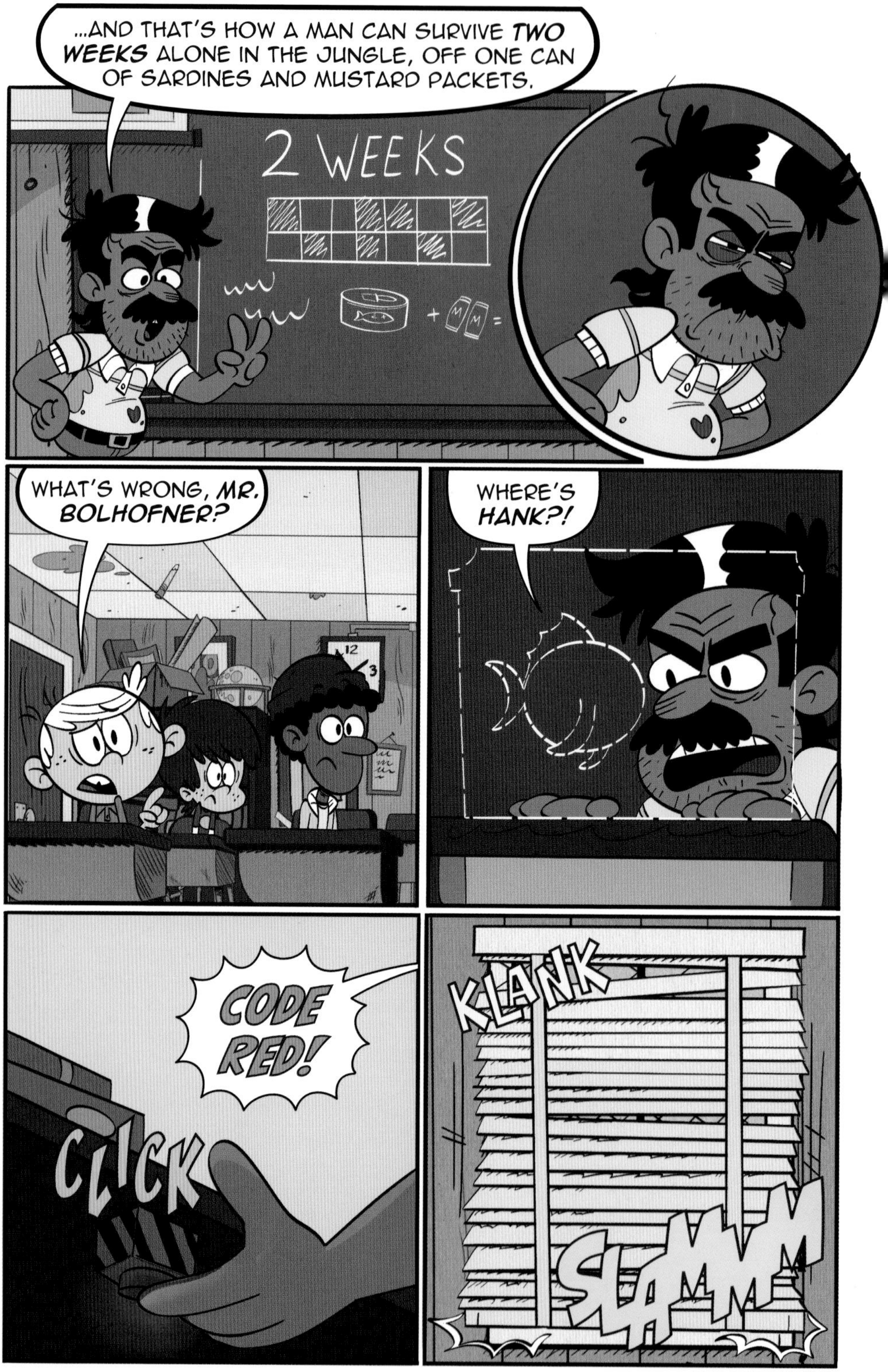

...AND THAT'S HOW A MAN CAN SURVIVE *TWO WEEKS* ALONE IN THE JUNGLE, OFF ONE CAN OF SARDINES AND MUSTARD PACKETS.
2 WEEKS
WHAT'S WRONG, *MR. BOLHOFNER?*
WHERE'S *HANK?!*
CODE RED!
CLICK
KLANK
SLAMMM

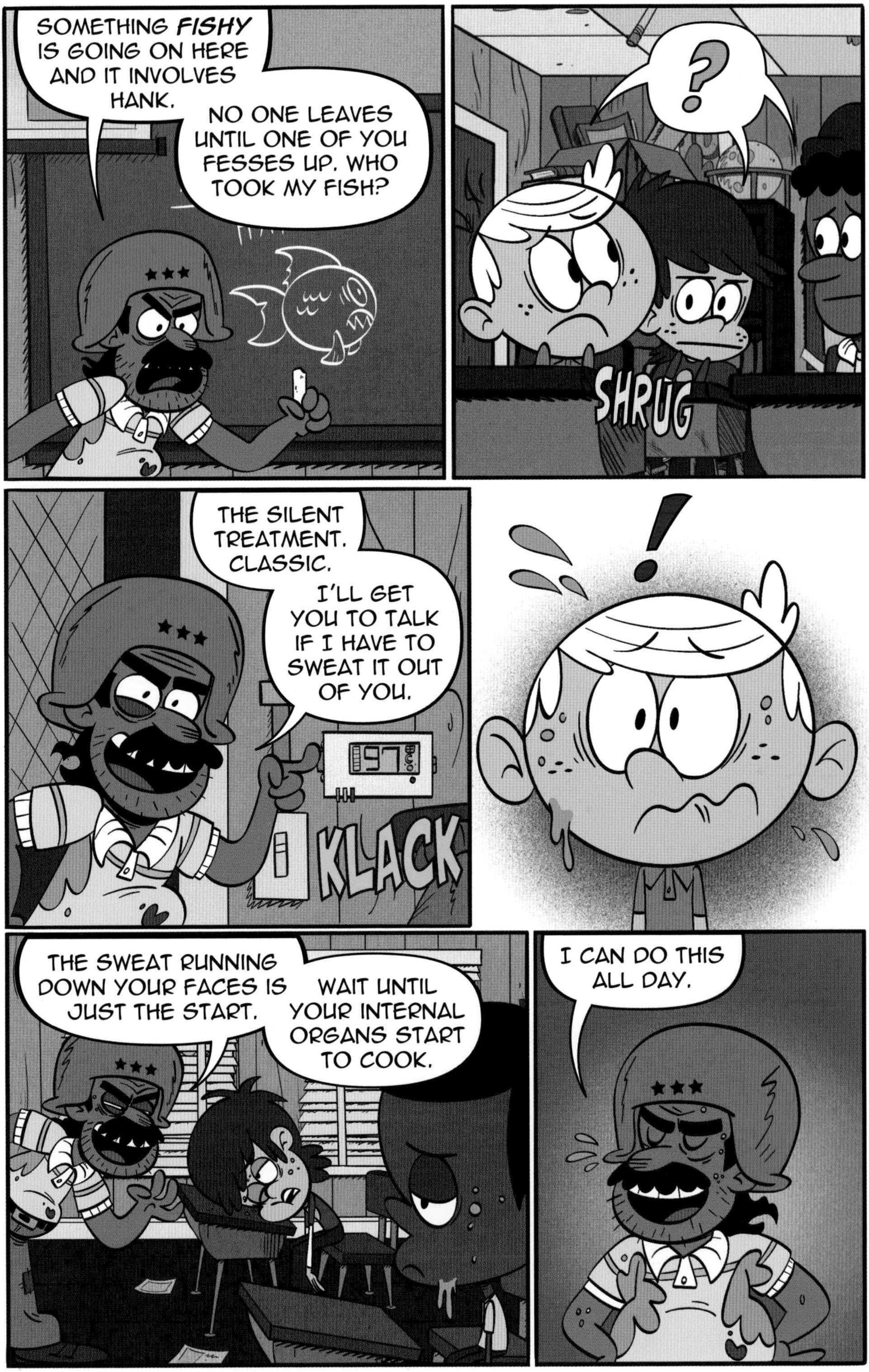
SOMETHING FISHY IS GOING ON HERE AND IT INVOLVES HANK.
NO ONE LEAVES UNTIL ONE OF YOU FESSES UP. WHO TOOK MY FISH?
?
SHRUG
THE SILENT TREATMENT. CLASSIC.
I'LL GET YOU TO TALK IF I HAVE TO SWEAT IT OUT OF YOU.
97
KLACK
!
THE SWEAT RUNNING DOWN YOUR FACES IS JUST THE START.
WAIT UNTIL YOUR INTERNAL ORGANS START TO COOK.
I CAN DO THIS ALL DAY.

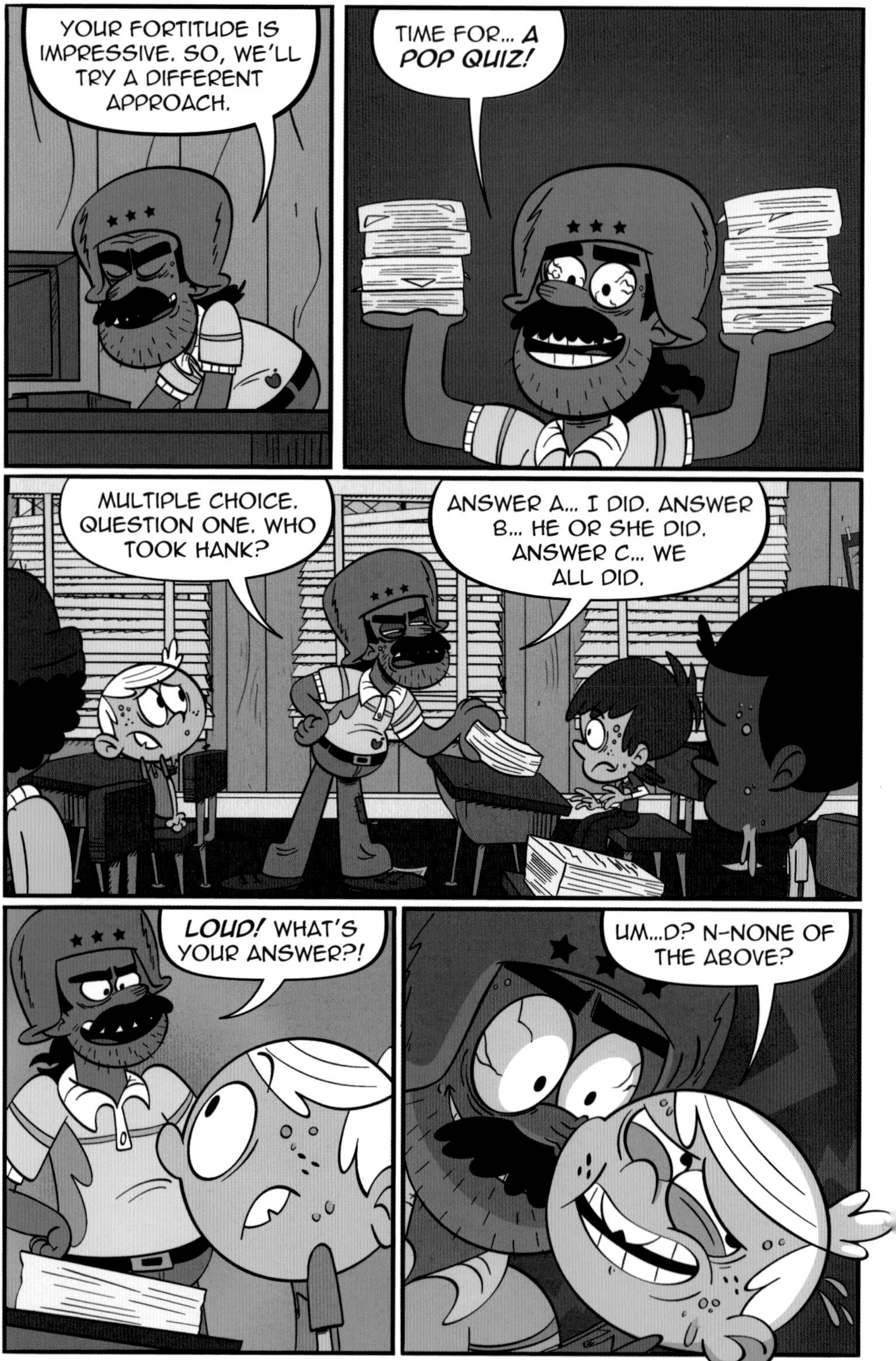
YOUR FORTITUDE IS IMPRESSIVE. SO, WE'LL TRY A DIFFERENT APPROACH.
TIME FOR... *A POP QUIZ!*
MULTIPLE CHOICE. QUESTION ONE. WHO TOOK HANK?
ANSWER A... I DID. ANSWER B... HE OR SHE DID. ANSWER C... WE ALL DID.
LOUD! WHAT'S YOUR ANSWER?!
UM...D? N-NONE OF THE ABOVE?

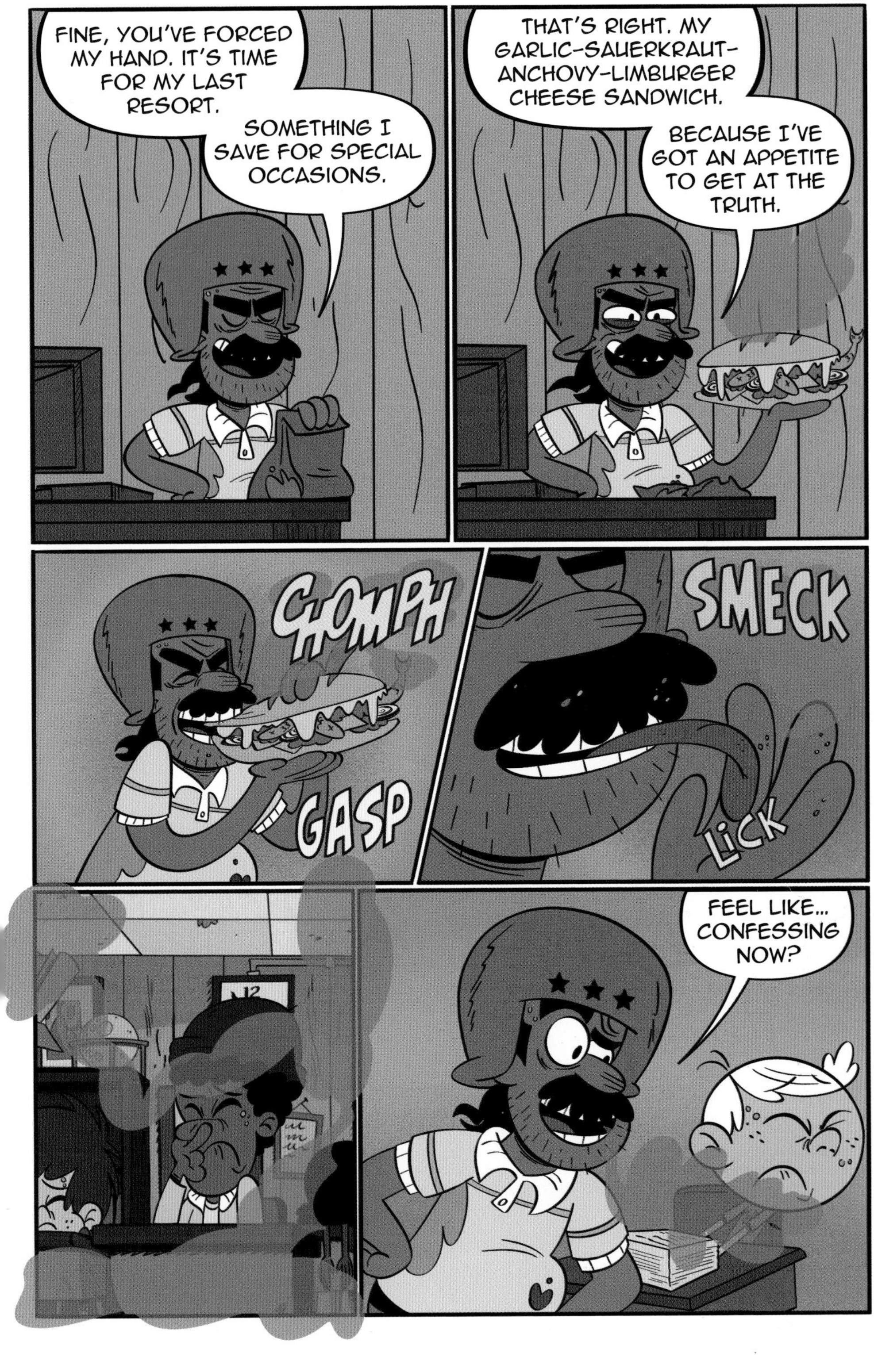
FINE, YOU'VE FORCED MY HAND. IT'S TIME FOR MY LAST RESORT.
SOMETHING I SAVE FOR SPECIAL OCCASIONS.
THAT'S RIGHT. MY GARLIC-SAUERKRAUT-ANCHOVY-LIMBURGER CHEESE SANDWICH.
BECAUSE I'VE GOT AN APPETITE TO GET AT THE TRUTH.
CHOMPH
GASP
SMECK
LICK
FEEL LIKE... CONFESSING NOW?

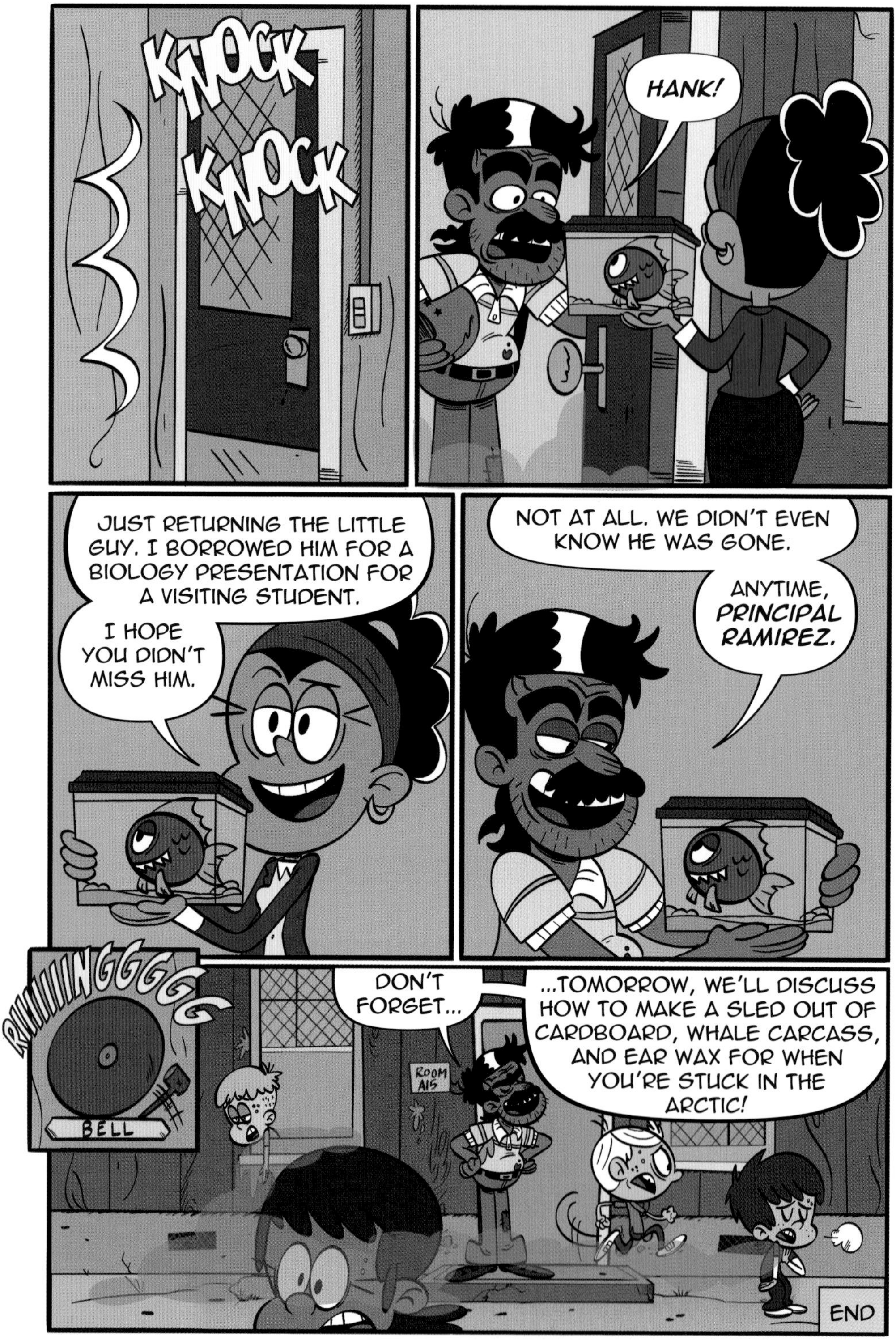
KNOCK KNOCK
HANK!
JUST RETURNING THE LITTLE GUY. I BORROWED HIM FOR A BIOLOGY PRESENTATION FOR A VISITING STUDENT.
I HOPE YOU DIDN'T MISS HIM.
NOT AT ALL. WE DIDN'T EVEN KNOW HE WAS GONE.
ANYTIME, PRINCIPAL RAMIREZ.
RIIIIIINGGGGG
BELL
ROOM A15
DON'T FORGET...
...TOMORROW, WE'LL DISCUSS HOW TO MAKE A SLED OUT OF CARDBOARD, WHALE CARCASS, AND EAR WAX FOR WHEN YOU'RE STUCK IN THE ARCTIC!
END

"TRENDFRETTER"

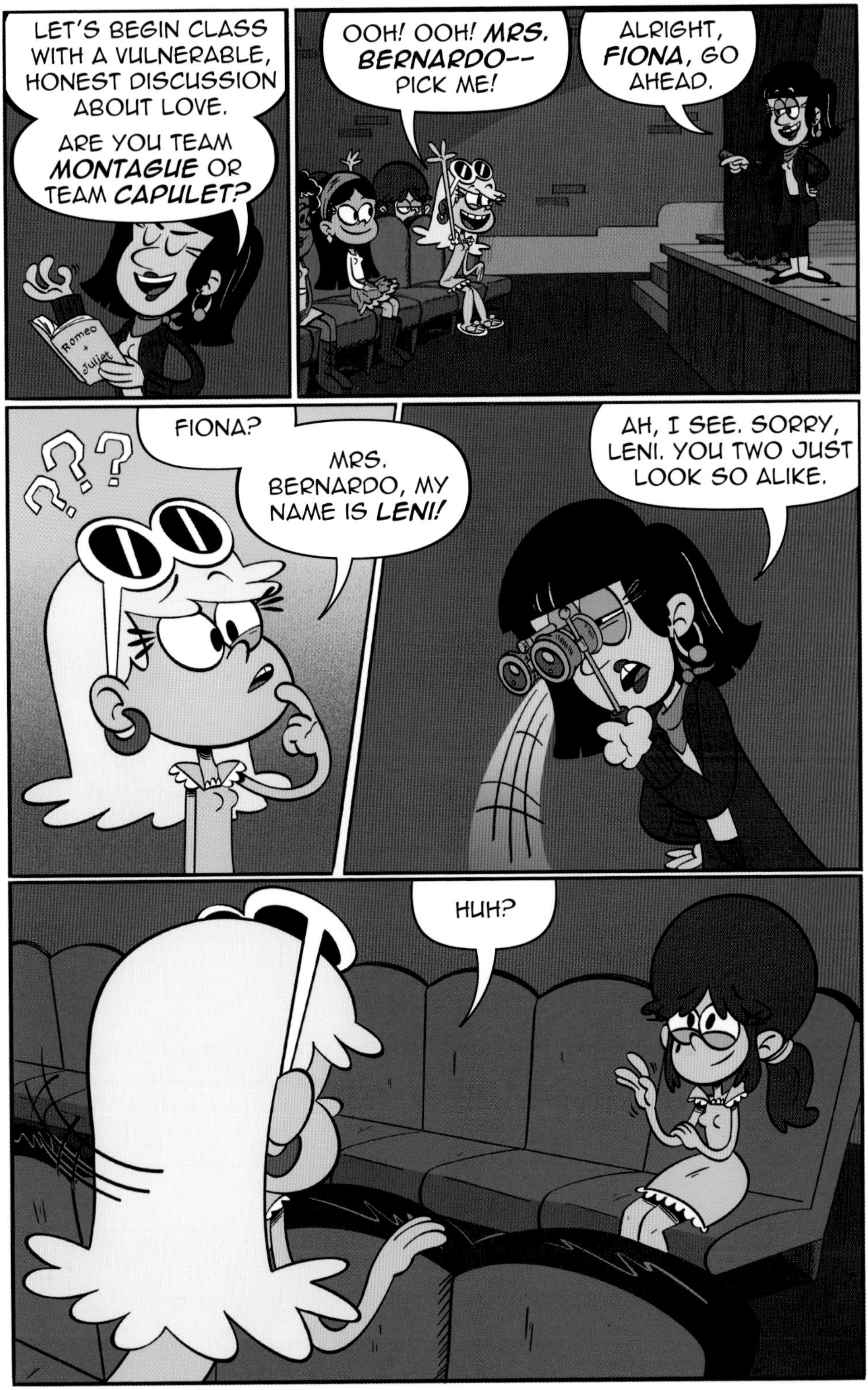

LET'S BEGIN CLASS WITH A VULNERABLE, HONEST DISCUSSION ABOUT LOVE.
ARE YOU TEAM MONTAGUE OR TEAM CAPULET?
Romeo + Juliet
OOH! OOH! MRS. BERNARDO-- PICK ME!
ALRIGHT, FIONA, GO AHEAD.
FIONA?
MRS. BERNARDO, MY NAME IS LENI!
AH, I SEE. SORRY, LENI. YOU TWO JUST LOOK SO ALIKE.
HUH?

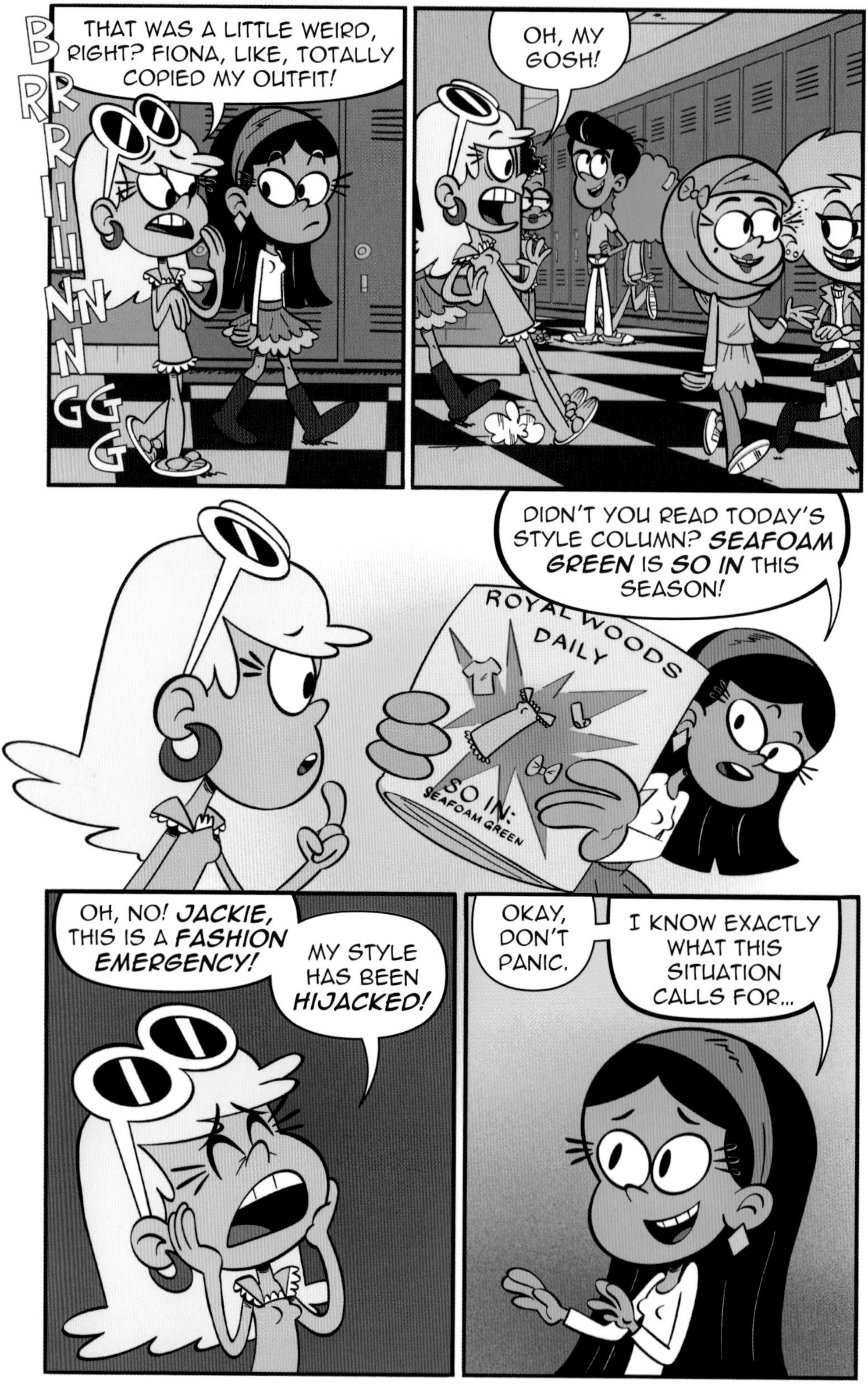
BRRRIIIINNNNGGG
THAT WAS A LITTLE WEIRD, RIGHT? FIONA, LIKE, TOTALLY COPIED MY OUTFIT!
OH, MY GOSH!
DIDN'T YOU READ TODAY'S STYLE COLUMN? SEAFOAM GREEN IS SO IN THIS SEASON!
ROYAL WOODS DAILY
SO IN: SEAFOAM GREEN
OH, NO! JACKIE, THIS IS A FASHION EMERGENCY!
MY STYLE HAS BEEN HIJACKED!
OKAY, DON'T PANIC.
I KNOW EXACTLY WHAT THIS SITUATION CALLS FOR...

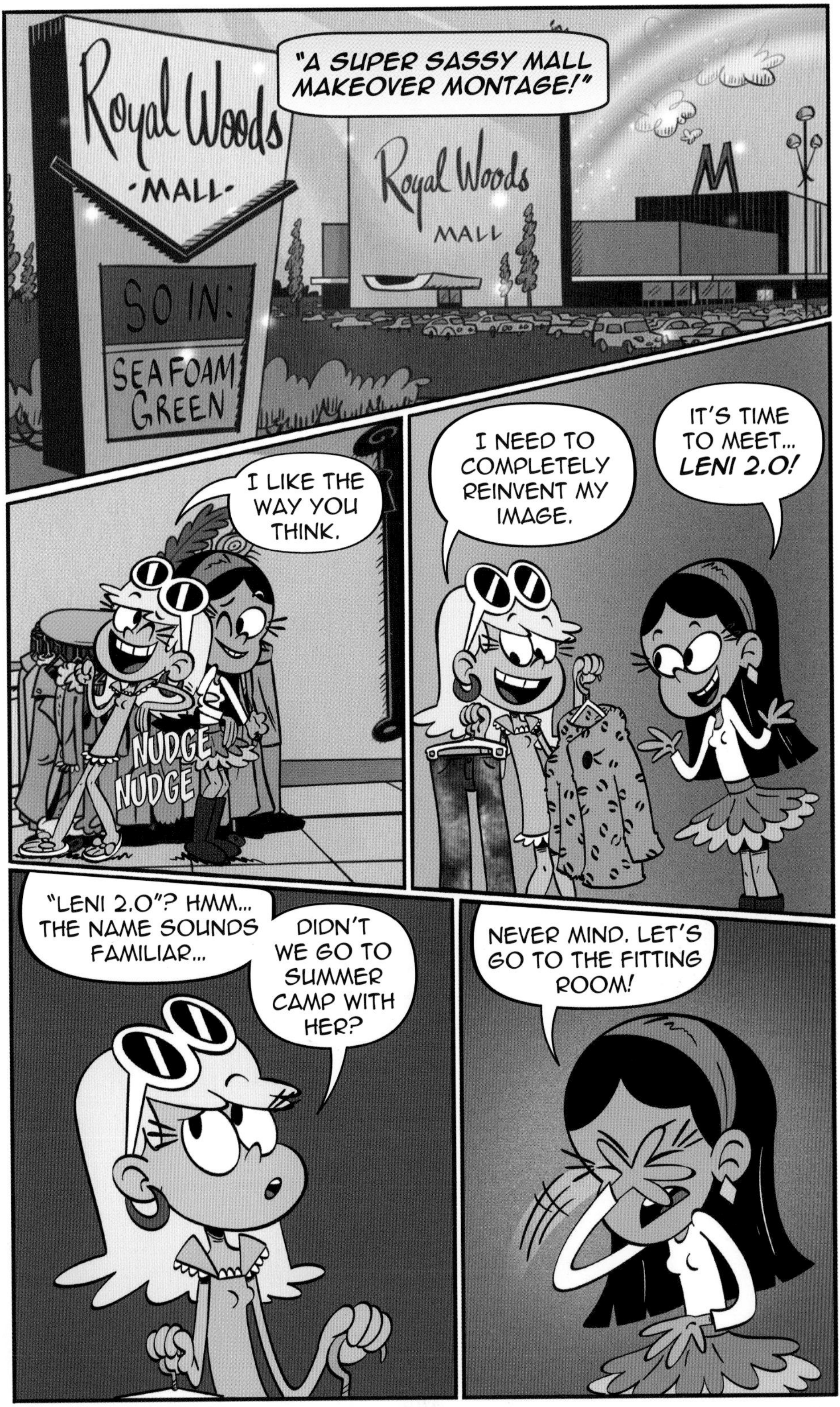
Royal Woods
·MALL·
SO IN:
SEAFOAM GREEN
"A SUPER SASSY MALL MAKEOVER MONTAGE!"
Royal Woods
MALL
I LIKE THE WAY YOU THINK.
NUDGE NUDGE
I NEED TO COMPLETELY REINVENT MY IMAGE.
IT'S TIME TO MEET... LENI 2.0!
"LENI 2.0"? HMM... THE NAME SOUNDS FAMILIAR...
DIDN'T WE GO TO SUMMER CAMP WITH HER?
NEVER MIND. LET'S GO TO THE FITTING ROOM!

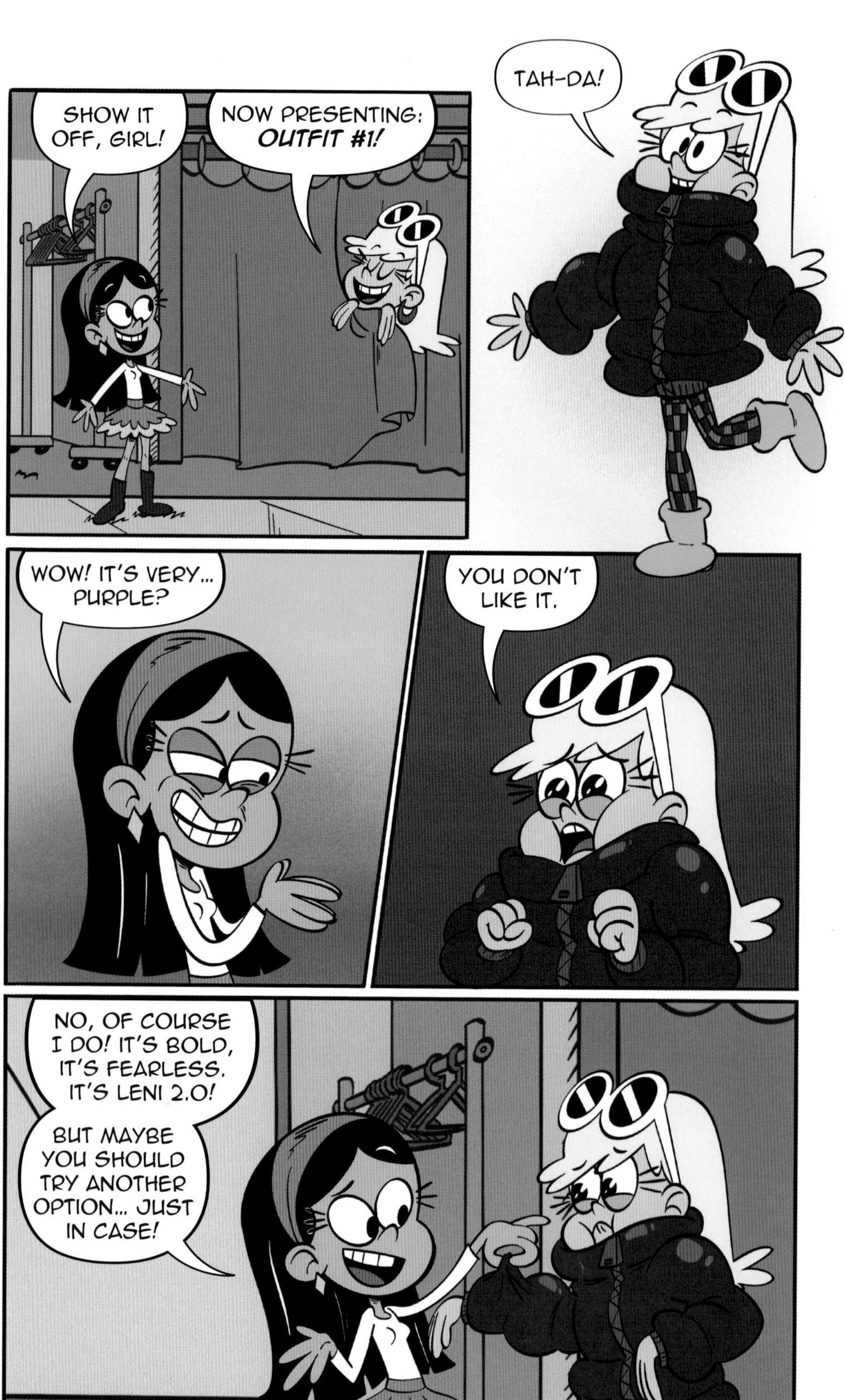
SHOW IT OFF, GIRL!
NOW PRESENTING: OUTFIT #1!
TAH-DA!
WOW! IT'S VERY... PURPLE?
YOU DON'T LIKE IT.
NO, OF COURSE I DO! IT'S BOLD, IT'S FEARLESS. IT'S LENI 2.0!
BUT MAYBE YOU SHOULD TRY ANOTHER OPTION... JUST IN CASE!

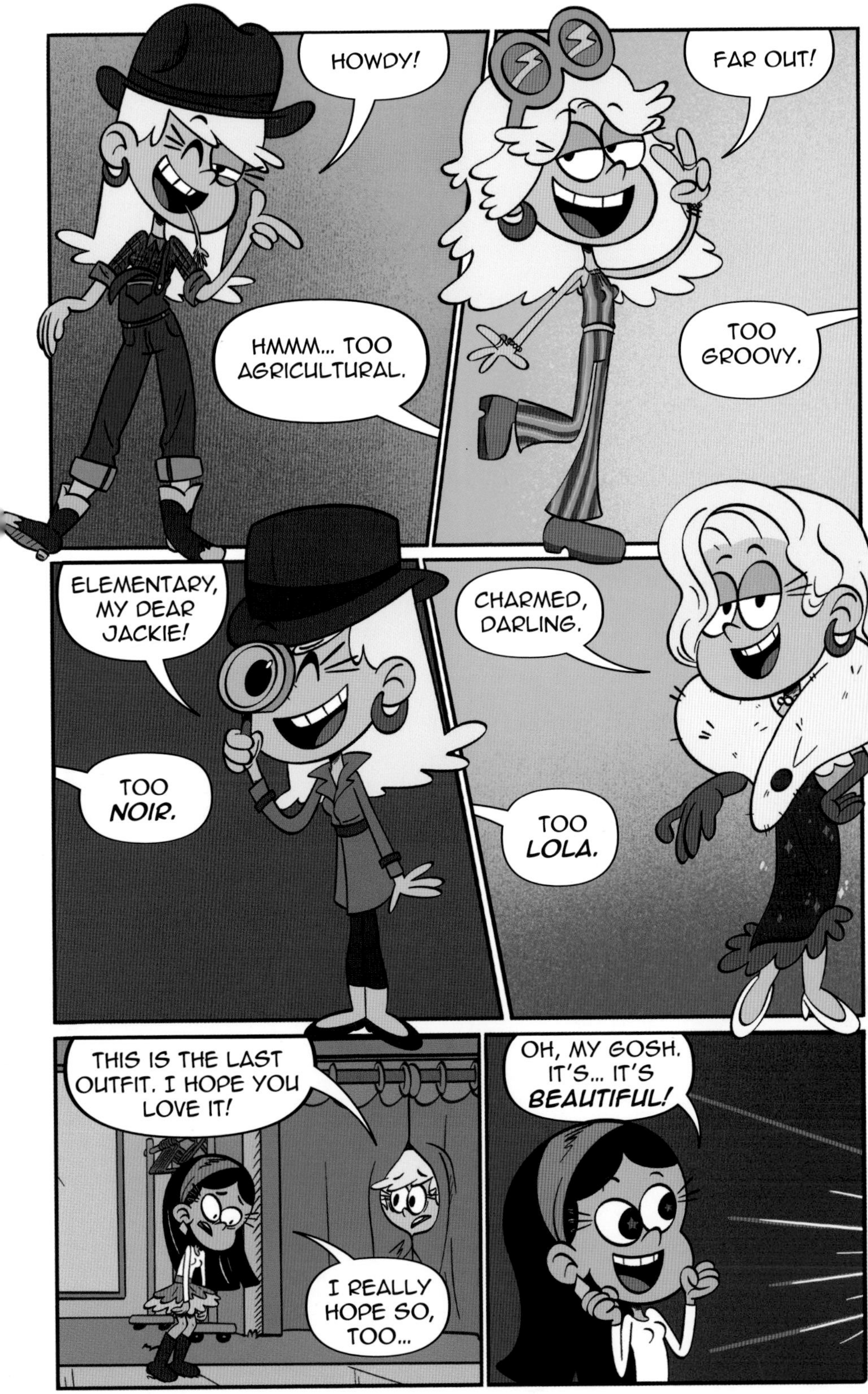
HOWDY!
FAR OUT!
HMMM... TOO AGRICULTURAL.
TOO GROOVY.
ELEMENTARY, MY DEAR JACKIE!
CHARMED, DARLING.
TOO *NOIR.*
TOO *LOLA.*
THIS IS THE LAST OUTFIT. I HOPE YOU LOVE IT!
I REALLY HOPE SO, TOO...
OH, MY GOSH. IT'S... IT'S *BEAUTIFUL!*

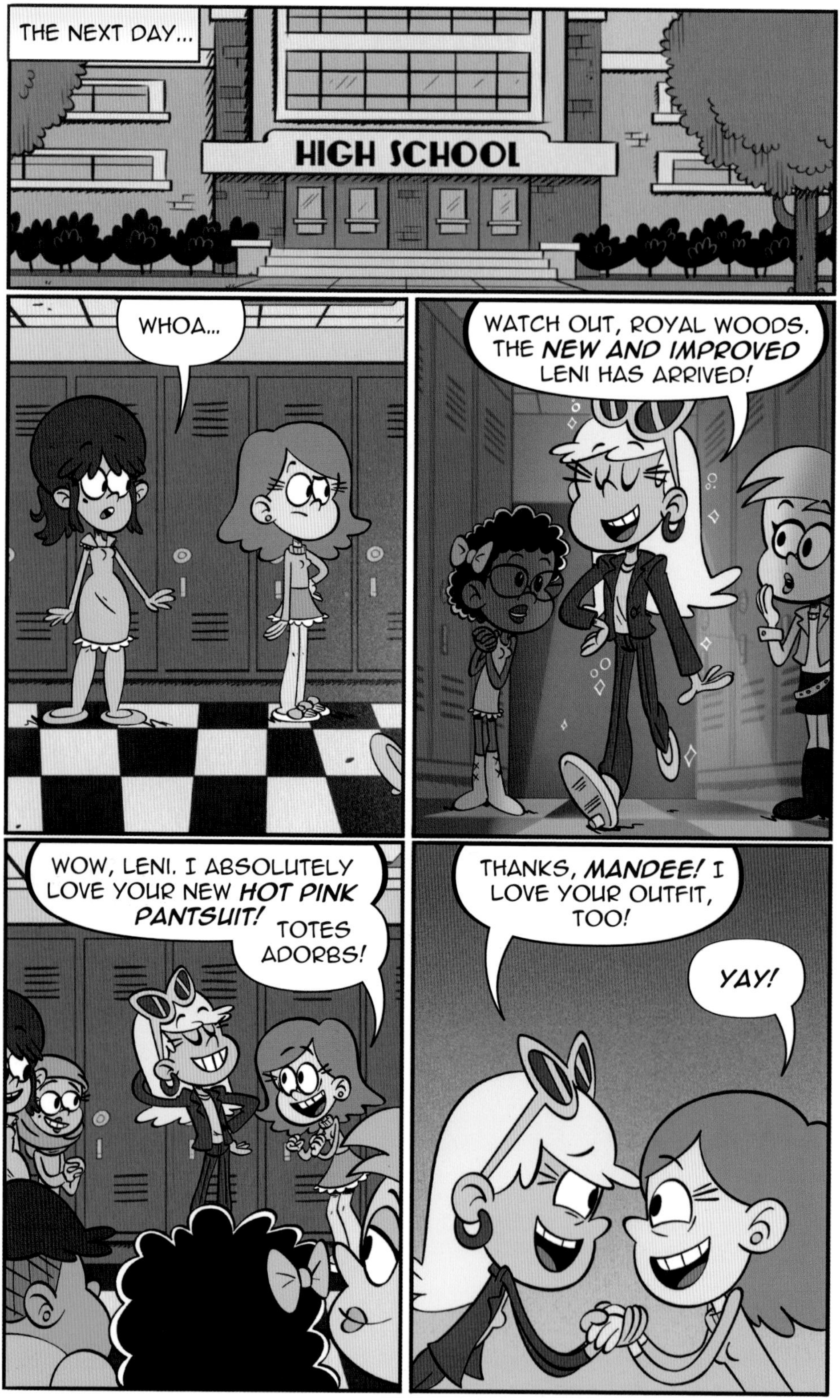
THE NEXT DAY...
HIGH SCHOOL
WHOA...
WATCH OUT, ROYAL WOODS. THE NEW AND IMPROVED LENI HAS ARRIVED!
WOW, LENI. I ABSOLUTELY LOVE YOUR NEW HOT PINK PANTSUIT!
TOTES ADORBS!
THANKS, MANDEE! I LOVE YOUR OUTFIT, TOO!
YAY!

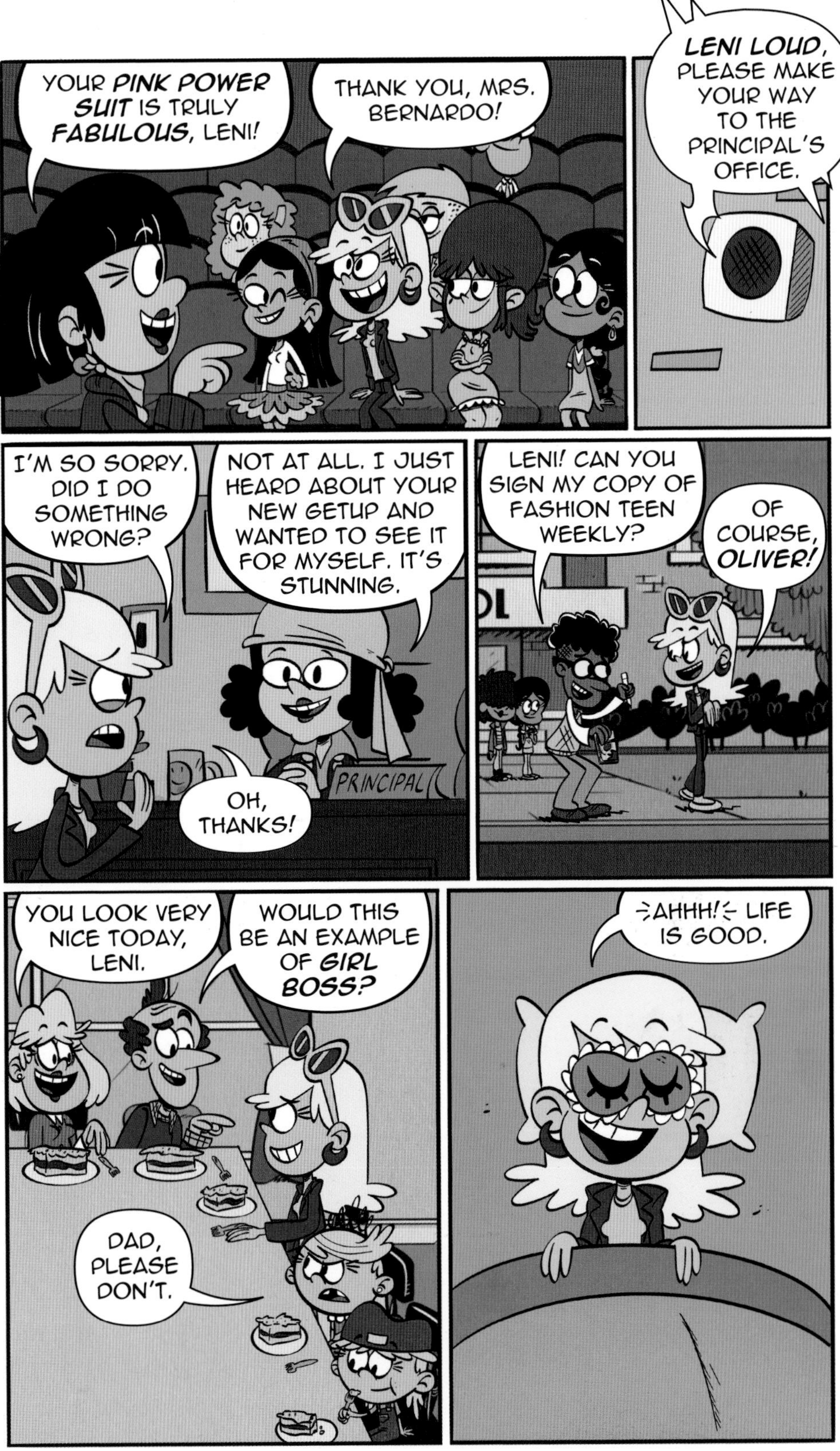
YOUR PINK POWER SUIT IS TRULY FABULOUS, LENI!
THANK YOU, MRS. BERNARDO!
LENI LOUD, PLEASE MAKE YOUR WAY TO THE PRINCIPAL'S OFFICE.
I'M SO SORRY. DID I DO SOMETHING WRONG?
NOT AT ALL. I JUST HEARD ABOUT YOUR NEW GETUP AND WANTED TO SEE IT FOR MYSELF. IT'S STUNNING.
OH, THANKS!
PRINCIPAL
LENI! CAN YOU SIGN MY COPY OF FASHION TEEN WEEKLY?
OF COURSE, OLIVER!
YOU LOOK VERY NICE TODAY, LENI.
WOULD THIS BE AN EXAMPLE OF GIRL BOSS?
DAD, PLEASE DON'T.
AHHH! LIFE IS GOOD.

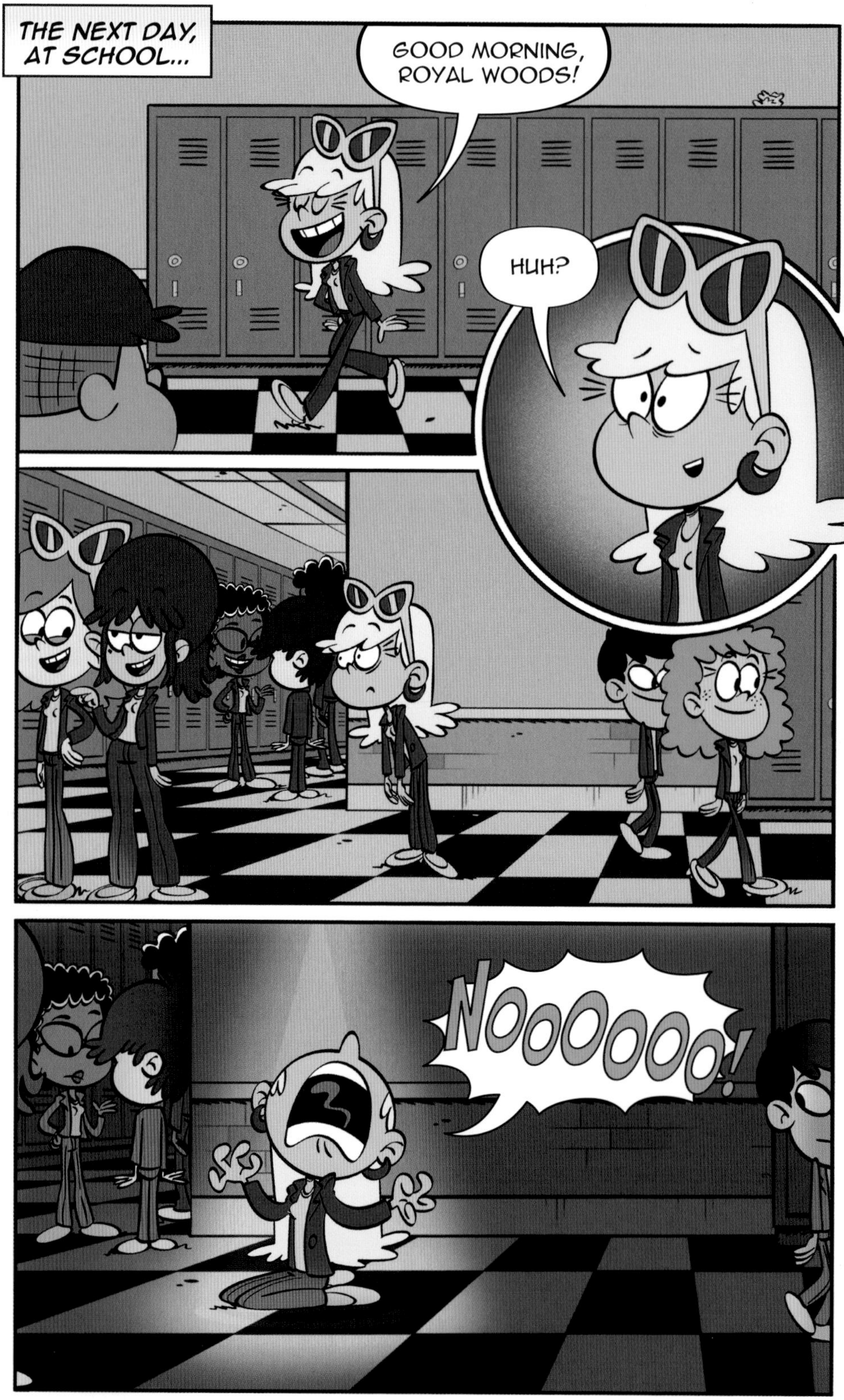
THE NEXT DAY, AT SCHOOL...
GOOD MORNING, ROYAL WOODS!
HUH?
NOOOOOO!

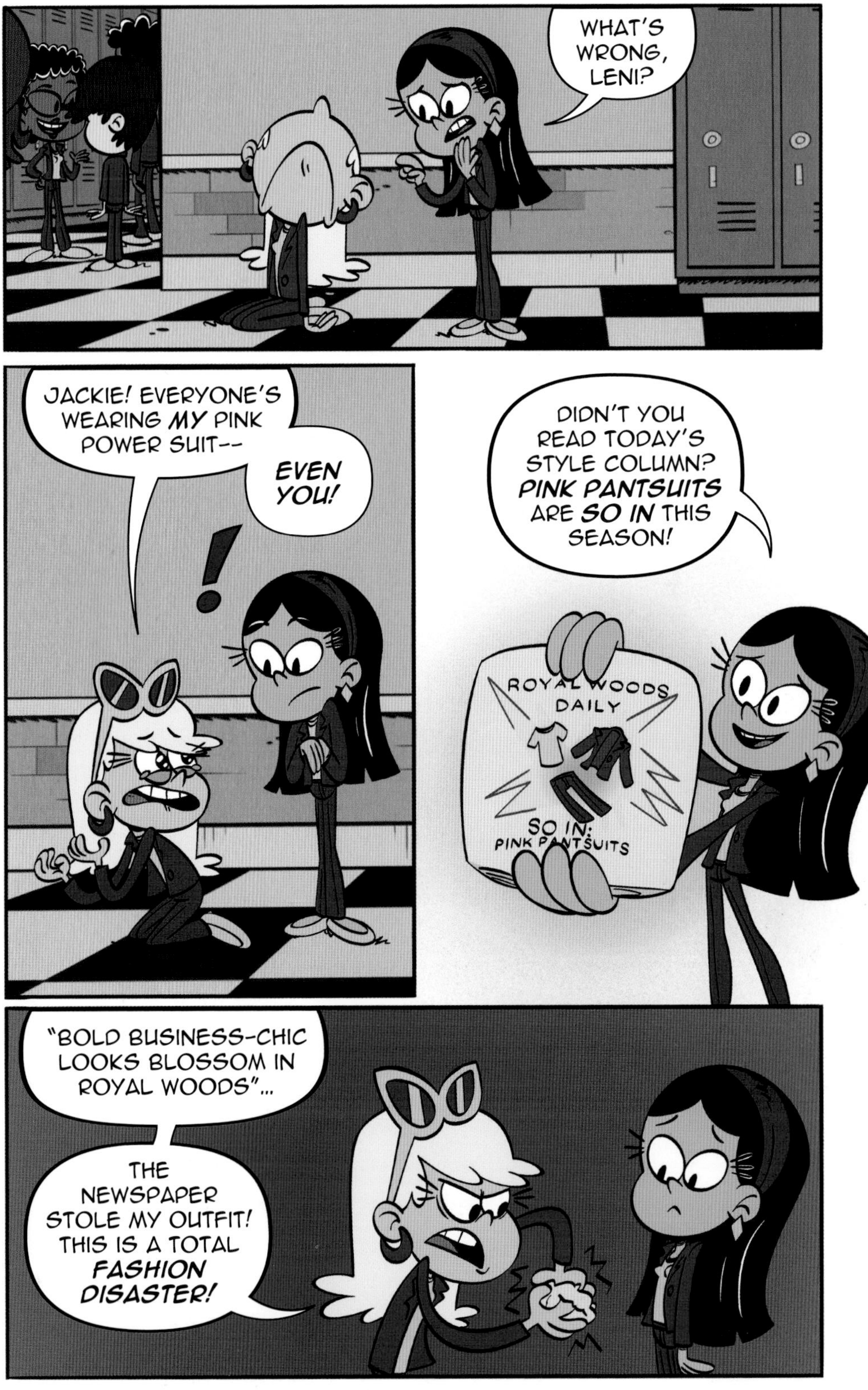
WHAT'S WRONG, LENI?
JACKIE! EVERYONE'S WEARING *MY* PINK POWER SUIT--
EVEN YOU!
!
DIDN'T YOU READ TODAY'S STYLE COLUMN? ***PINK PANTSUITS*** ARE ***SO IN*** THIS SEASON!
ROYAL WOODS DAILY
SO IN: PINK PANTSUITS
"BOLD BUSINESS-CHIC LOOKS BLOSSOM IN ROYAL WOODS"...
THE NEWSPAPER STOLE MY OUTFIT! THIS IS A TOTAL ***FASHION DISASTER!***

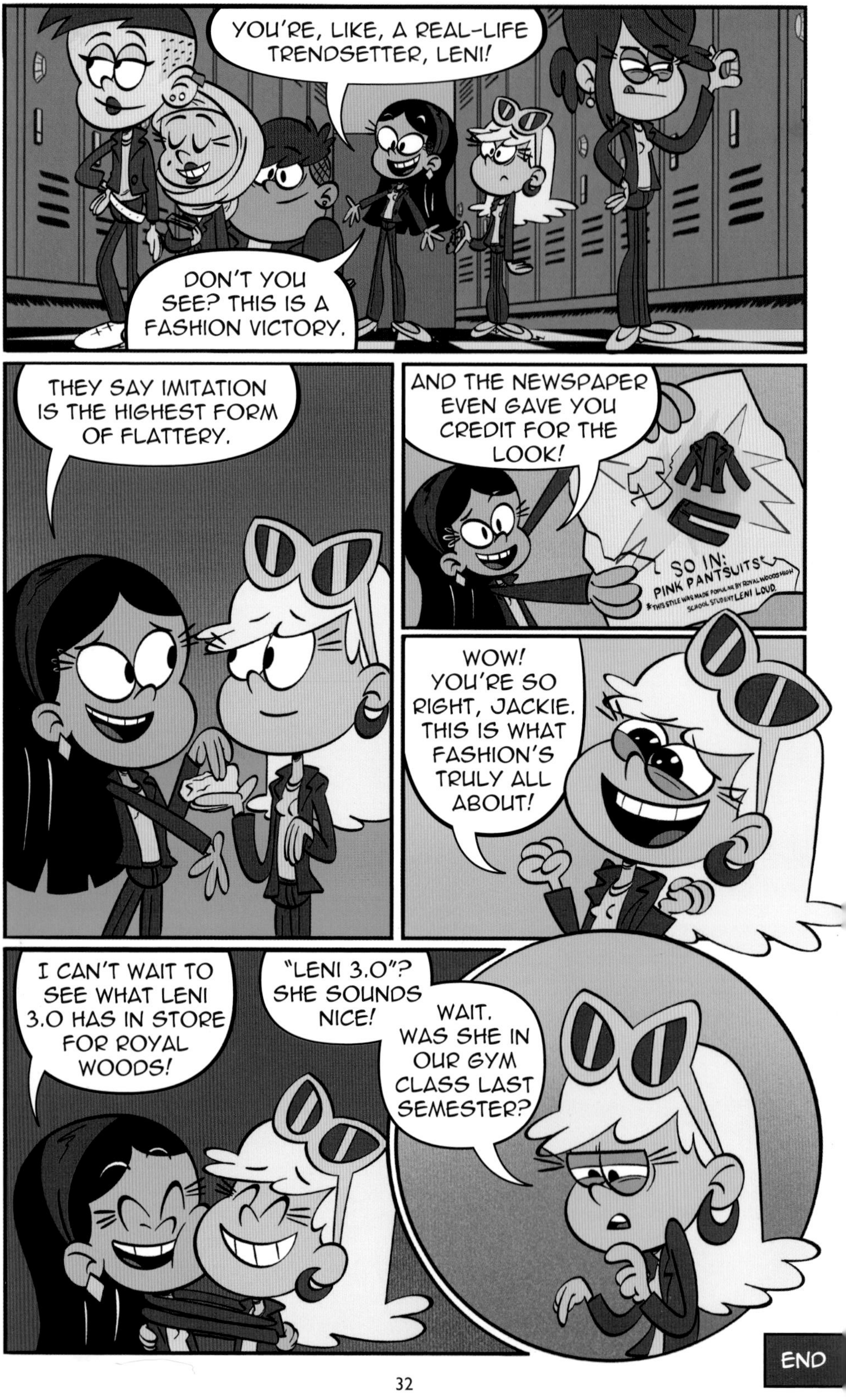
YOU'RE, LIKE, A REAL-LIFE TRENDSETTER, LENI!
DON'T YOU SEE? THIS IS A FASHION VICTORY.
THEY SAY IMITATION IS THE HIGHEST FORM OF FLATTERY.
AND THE NEWSPAPER EVEN GAVE YOU CREDIT FOR THE LOOK!
SO IN:
PINK PANTSUITS*
*THIS STYLE WAS MADE POPULAR BY ROYAL WOODS HIGH SCHOOL STUDENT LENI LOUD.
WOW! YOU'RE SO RIGHT, JACKIE. THIS IS WHAT FASHION'S TRULY ALL ABOUT!
I CAN'T WAIT TO SEE WHAT LENI 3.0 HAS IN STORE FOR ROYAL WOODS!
"LENI 3.0"? SHE SOUNDS NICE!
WAIT. WAS SHE IN OUR GYM CLASS LAST SEMESTER?
END

"LYNN IT TO WIN IT"

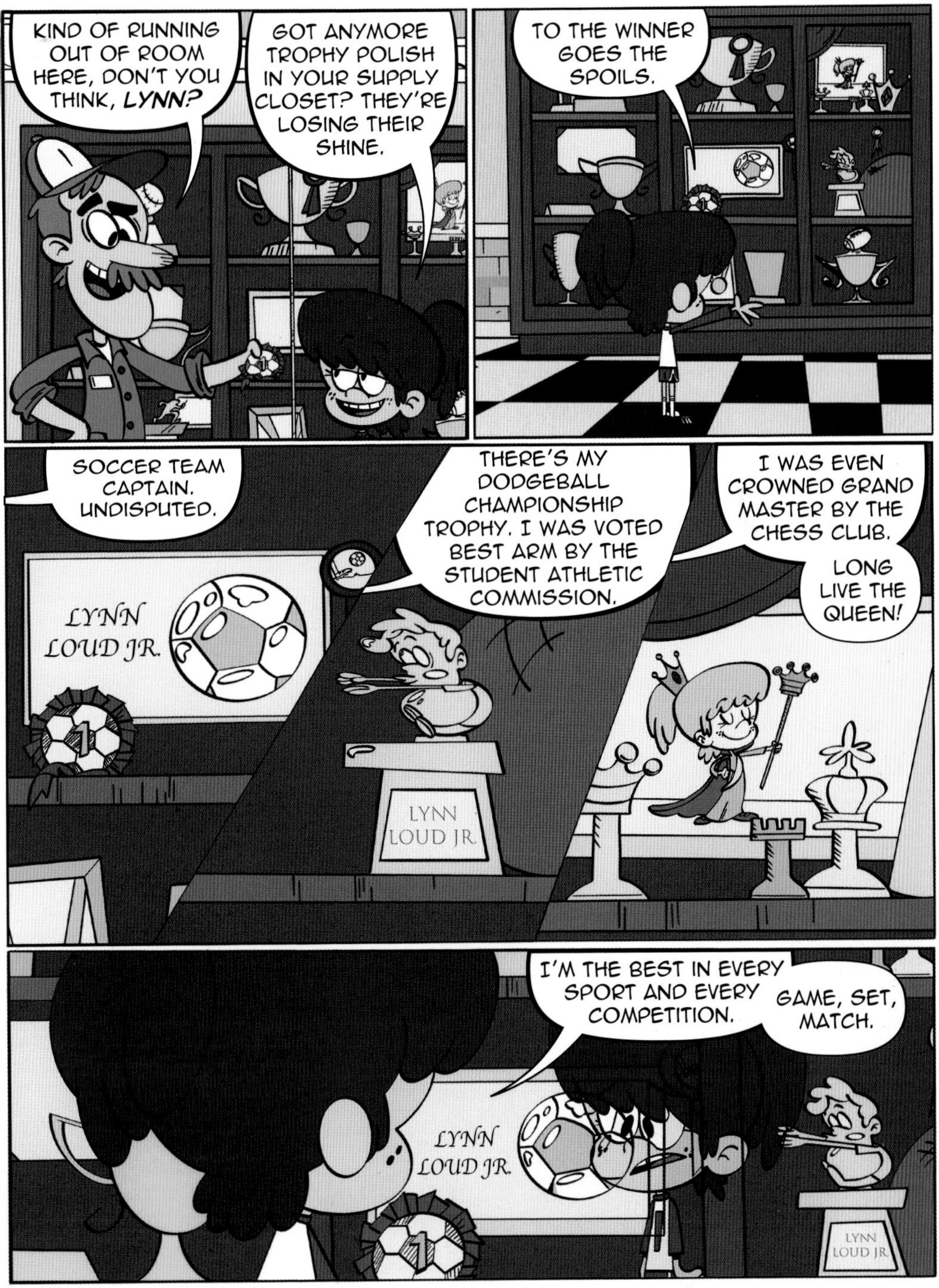

KIND OF RUNNING OUT OF ROOM HERE, DON'T YOU THINK, *LYNN?*
GOT ANYMORE TROPHY POLISH IN YOUR SUPPLY CLOSET? THEY'RE LOSING THEIR SHINE.
TO THE WINNER GOES THE SPOILS.
SOCCER TEAM CAPTAIN. UNDISPUTED.
LYNN LOUD JR.
THERE'S MY DODGEBALL CHAMPIONSHIP TROPHY. I WAS VOTED BEST ARM BY THE STUDENT ATHLETIC COMMISSION.
LYNN LOUD JR.
I WAS EVEN CROWNED GRAND MASTER BY THE CHESS CLUB.
LONG LIVE THE QUEEN!
I'M THE BEST IN EVERY SPORT AND EVERY COMPETITION.
GAME, SET, MATCH.
LYNN LOUD JR.
LYNN LOUD JR.

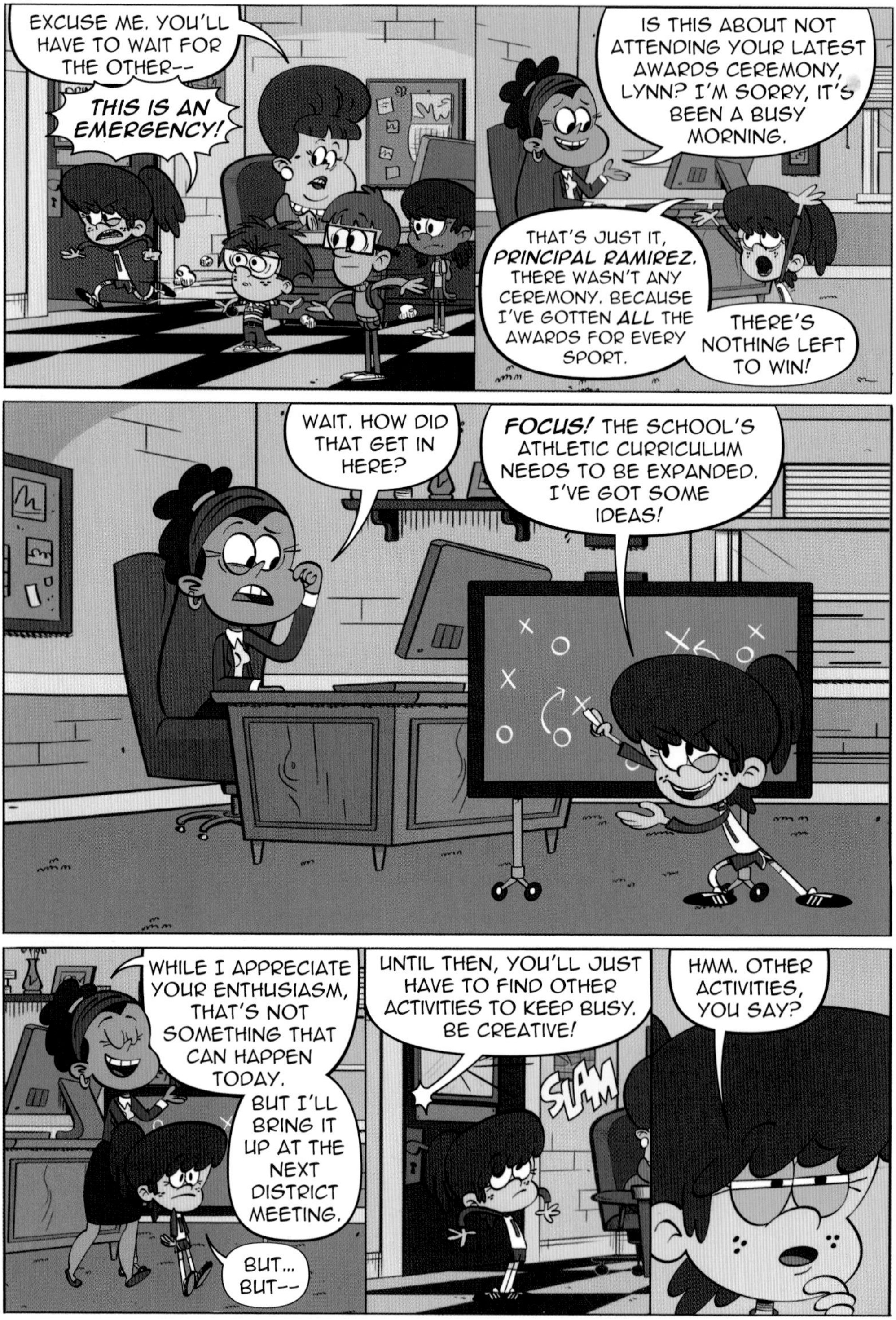

EXCUSE ME. YOU'LL HAVE TO WAIT FOR THE OTHER--
THIS IS AN EMERGENCY!
IS THIS ABOUT NOT ATTENDING YOUR LATEST AWARDS CEREMONY, LYNN? I'M SORRY, IT'S BEEN A BUSY MORNING.
THAT'S JUST IT, PRINCIPAL RAMIREZ. THERE WASN'T ANY CEREMONY. BECAUSE I'VE GOTTEN ALL THE AWARDS FOR EVERY SPORT.
THERE'S NOTHING LEFT TO WIN!
WAIT. HOW DID THAT GET IN HERE?
FOCUS! THE SCHOOL'S ATHLETIC CURRICULUM NEEDS TO BE EXPANDED. I'VE GOT SOME IDEAS!
WHILE I APPRECIATE YOUR ENTHUSIASM, THAT'S NOT SOMETHING THAT CAN HAPPEN TODAY.
BUT I'LL BRING IT UP AT THE NEXT DISTRICT MEETING.
BUT... BUT--
UNTIL THEN, YOU'LL JUST HAVE TO FIND OTHER ACTIVITIES TO KEEP BUSY. BE CREATIVE!
SLAM
HMM. OTHER ACTIVITIES, YOU SAY?

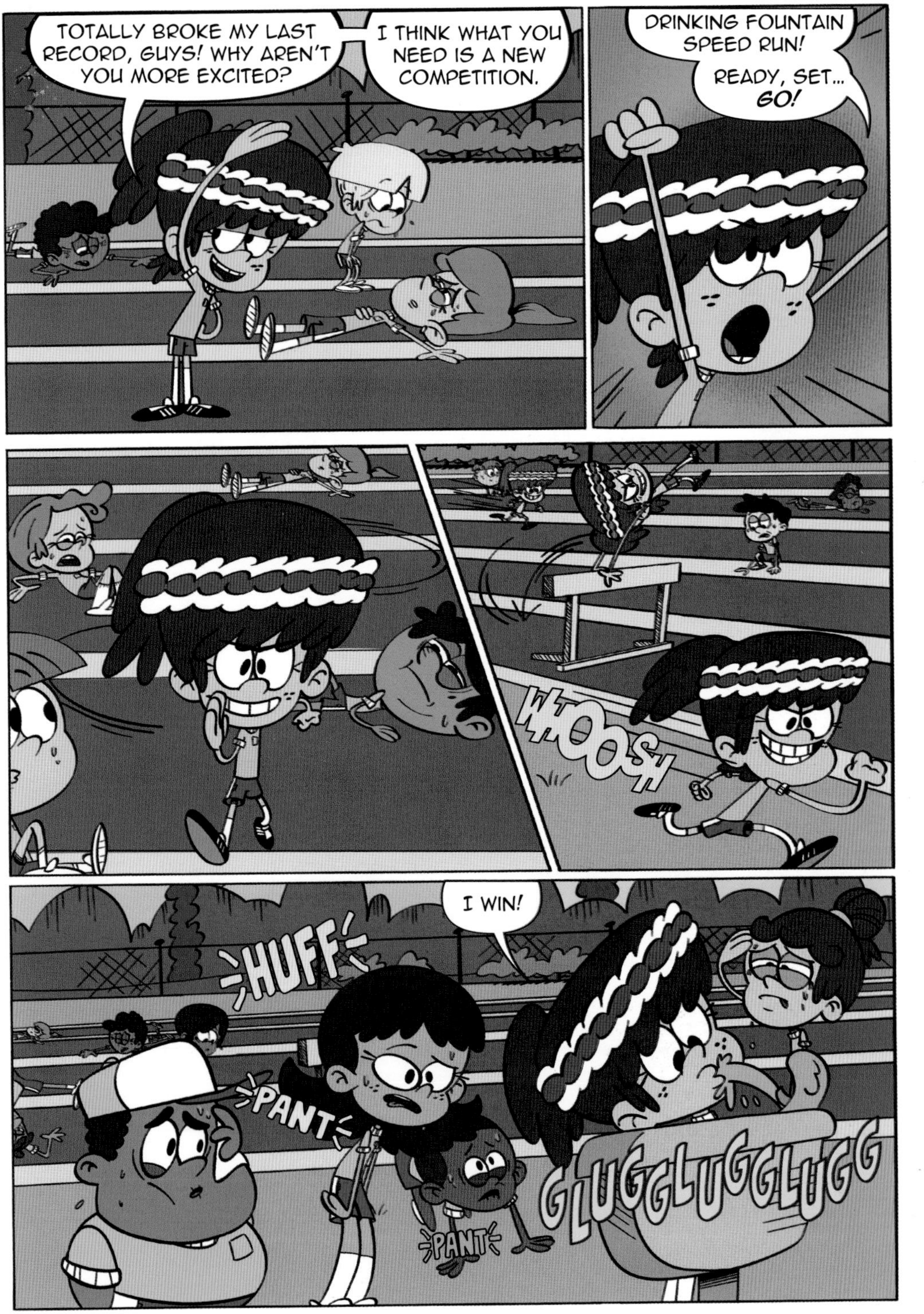
TOTALLY BROKE MY LAST RECORD, GUYS! WHY AREN'T YOU MORE EXCITED?
I THINK WHAT YOU NEED IS A NEW COMPETITION.
DRINKING FOUNTAIN SPEED RUN!
READY, SET... GO!
WOOSH
I WIN!
HUFF
PANT
PANT
GLUGGLUGGLUGG

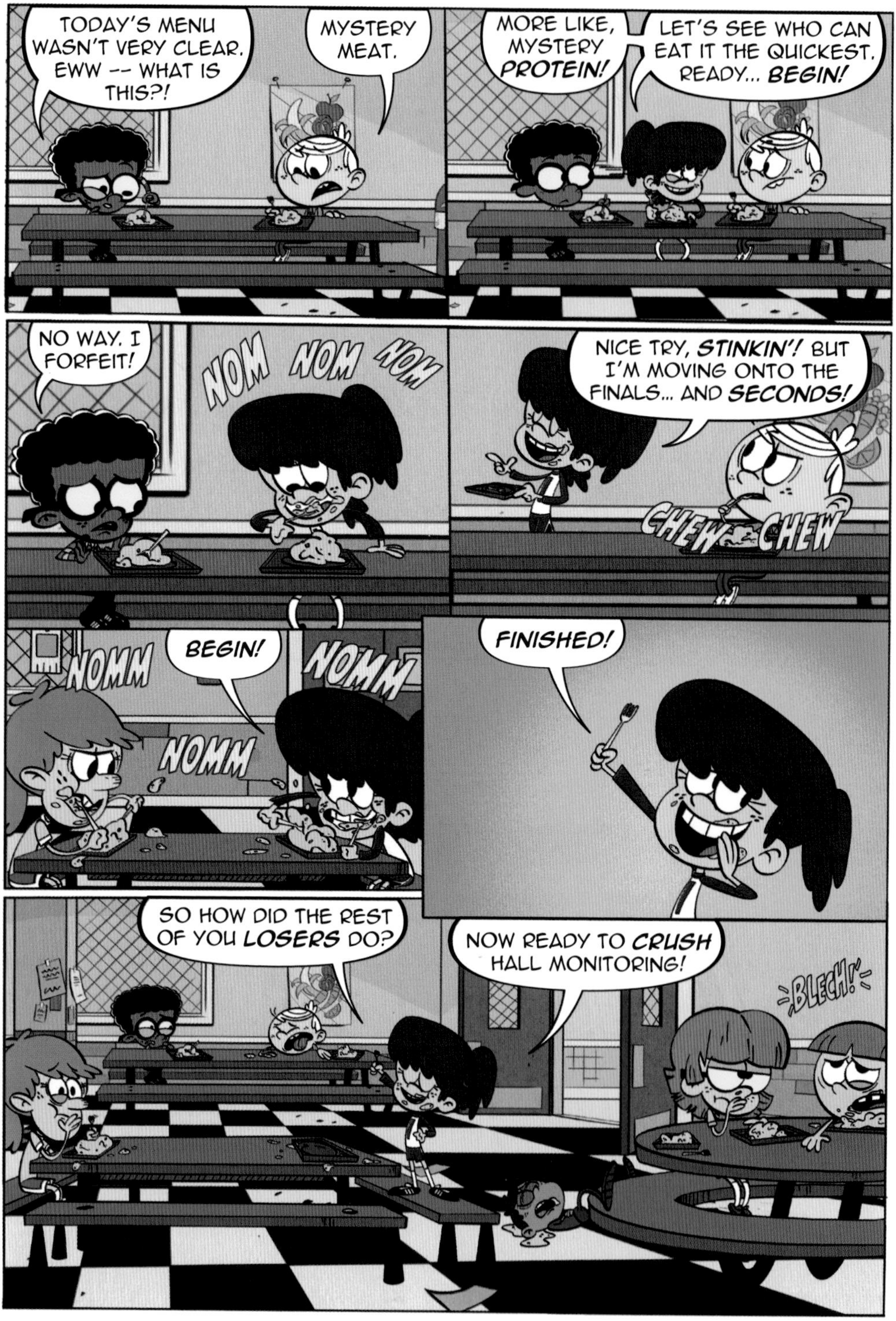
TODAY'S MENU WASN'T VERY CLEAR. EWW -- WHAT IS THIS?!
MYSTERY MEAT.
MORE LIKE, MYSTERY PROTEIN!
LET'S SEE WHO CAN EAT IT THE QUICKEST. READY... BEGIN!
NO WAY. I FORFEIT!
NOM NOM NOM
NICE TRY, STINKIN'! BUT I'M MOVING ONTO THE FINALS... AND SECONDS!
CHEW CHEW
NOMM
BEGIN!
NOMM
NOMM
FINISHED!
SO HOW DID THE REST OF YOU LOSERS DO?
NOW READY TO CRUSH HALL MONITORING!
BLECH!

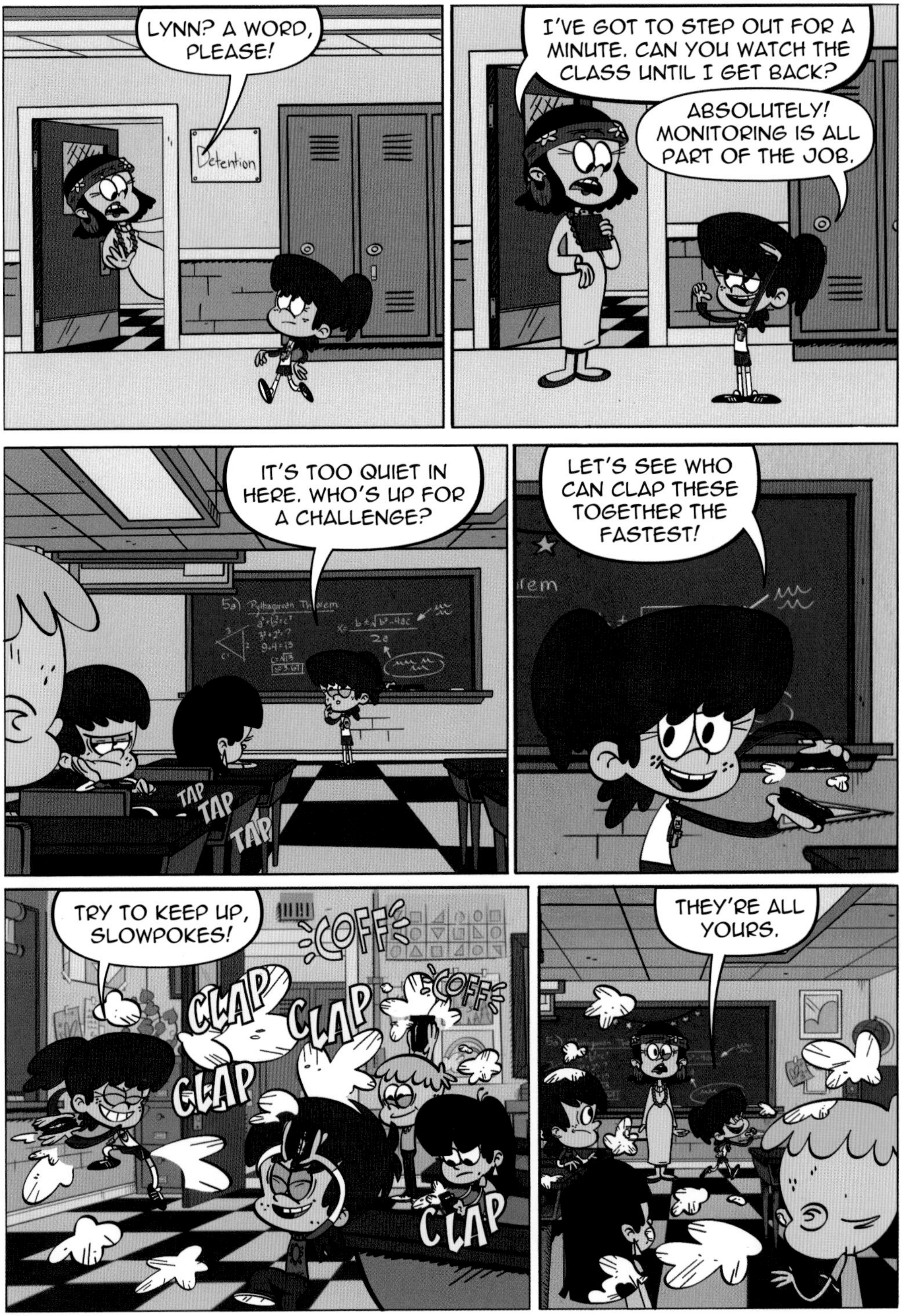
LYNN? A WORD, PLEASE!
Detention
I'VE GOT TO STEP OUT FOR A MINUTE. CAN YOU WATCH THE CLASS UNTIL I GET BACK?
ABSOLUTELY! MONITORING IS ALL PART OF THE JOB.
IT'S TOO QUIET IN HERE. WHO'S UP FOR A CHALLENGE?
Pythagorean Theorem
TAP
TAP
TAP
LET'S SEE WHO CAN CLAP THESE TOGETHER THE FASTEST!
TRY TO KEEP UP, SLOWPOKES!
COFF
CLAP
CLAP
COFF
CLAP
CLAP
THEY'RE ALL YOURS.

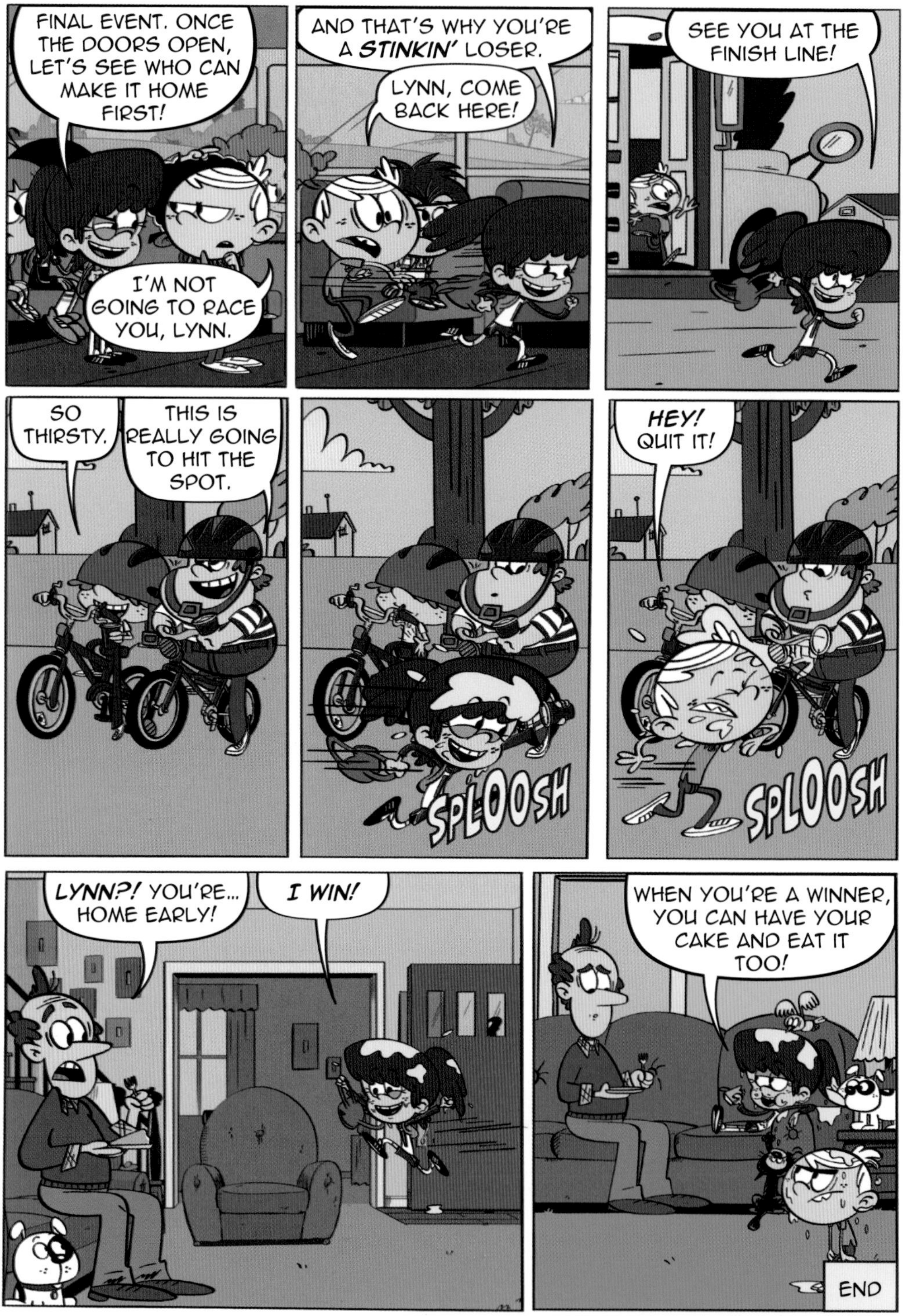
FINAL EVENT. ONCE THE DOORS OPEN, LET'S SEE WHO CAN MAKE IT HOME FIRST!
I'M NOT GOING TO RACE YOU, LYNN.
AND THAT'S WHY YOU'RE A STINKIN' LOSER.
LYNN, COME BACK HERE!
SEE YOU AT THE FINISH LINE!
SO THIRSTY.
THIS IS REALLY GOING TO HIT THE SPOT.
SPLOOSH
HEY! QUIT IT!
SPLOOSH
LYNN?! YOU'RE... HOME EARLY!
I WIN!
WHEN YOU'RE A WINNER, YOU CAN HAVE YOUR CAKE AND EAT IT TOO!
END

"ROCK N' ROLE MODEL"

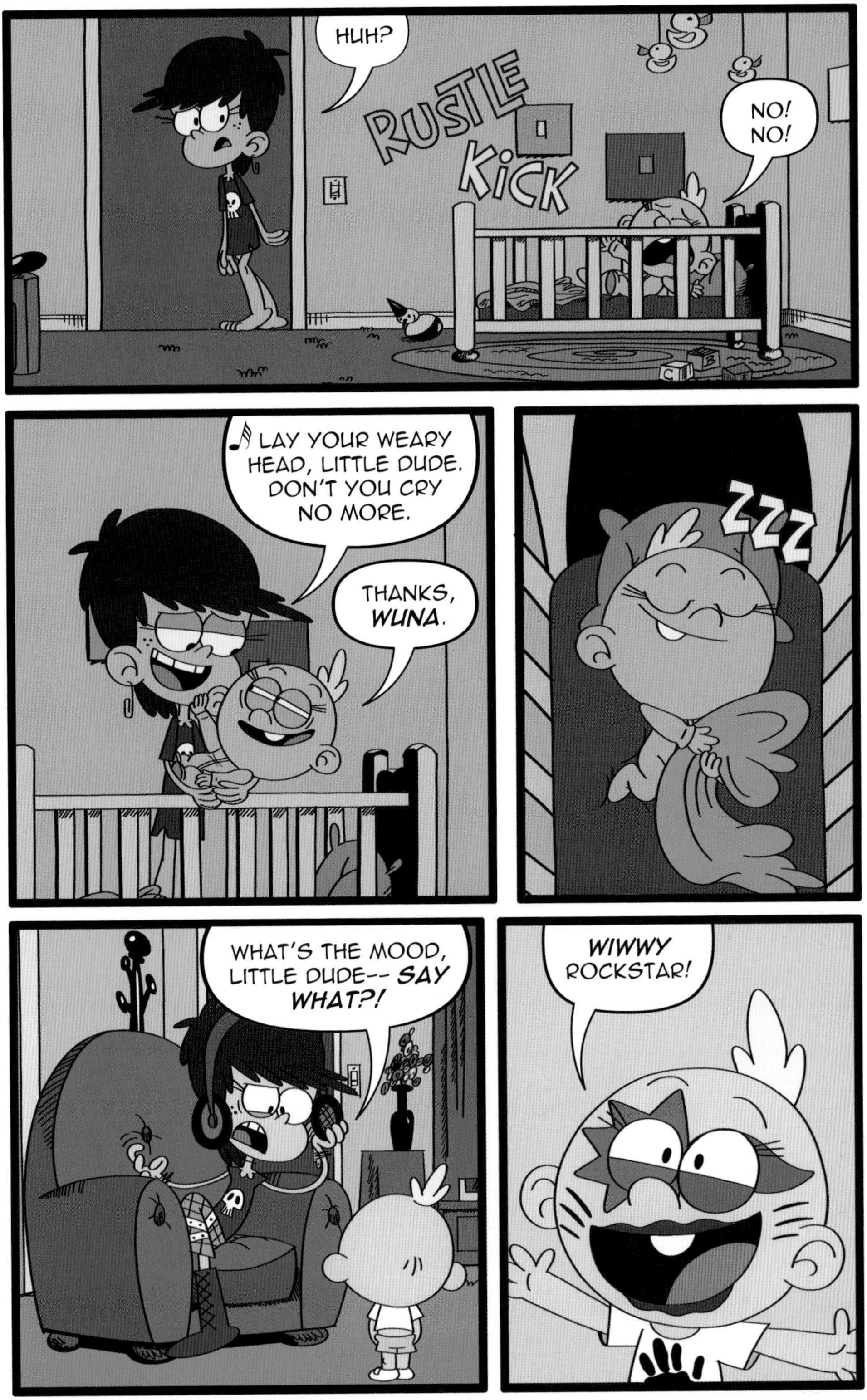
HUH?
RUSTLE
KICK
NO! NO!
LAY YOUR WEARY HEAD, LITTLE DUDE. DON'T YOU CRY NO MORE.
THANKS, *WUNA*.
ZZZ
WHAT'S THE MOOD, LITTLE DUDE-- *SAY WHAT?!*
WIWWY ROCKSTAR!

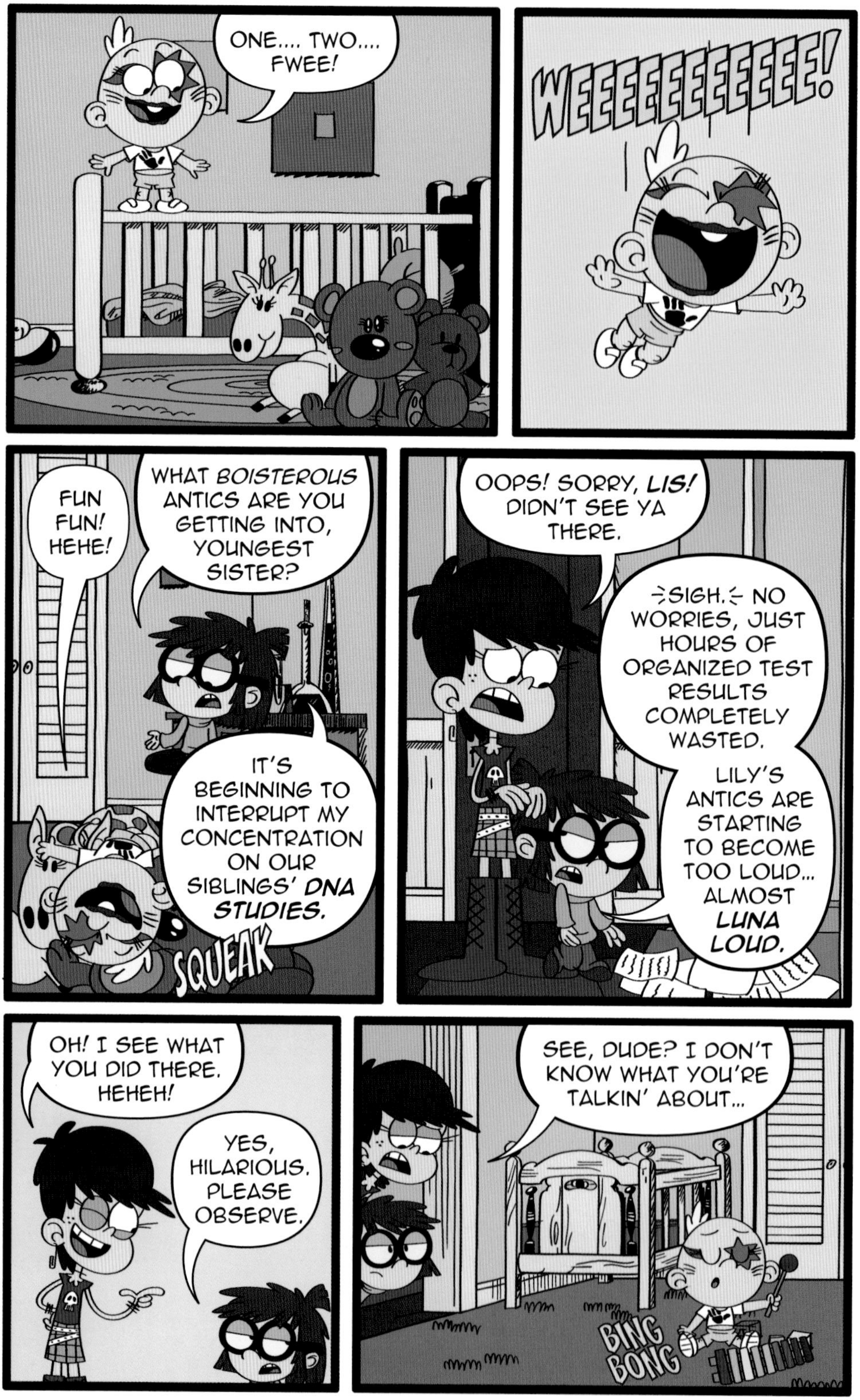

ONE.... TWO.... FWEE!
WEEEEEEEEEEE!
FUN FUN! HEHE!
WHAT BOISTEROUS ANTICS ARE YOU GETTING INTO, YOUNGEST SISTER?
IT'S BEGINNING TO INTERRUPT MY CONCENTRATION ON OUR SIBLINGS' DNA STUDIES.
SQUEAK
OOPS! SORRY, LIS! DIDN'T SEE YA THERE.
SIGH. NO WORRIES, JUST HOURS OF ORGANIZED TEST RESULTS COMPLETELY WASTED.
LILY'S ANTICS ARE STARTING TO BECOME TOO LOUD... ALMOST LUNA LOUD.
OH! I SEE WHAT YOU DID THERE. HEHEH!
YES, HILARIOUS. PLEASE OBSERVE.
SEE, DUDE? I DON'T KNOW WHAT YOU'RE TALKIN' ABOUT...
BING BONG

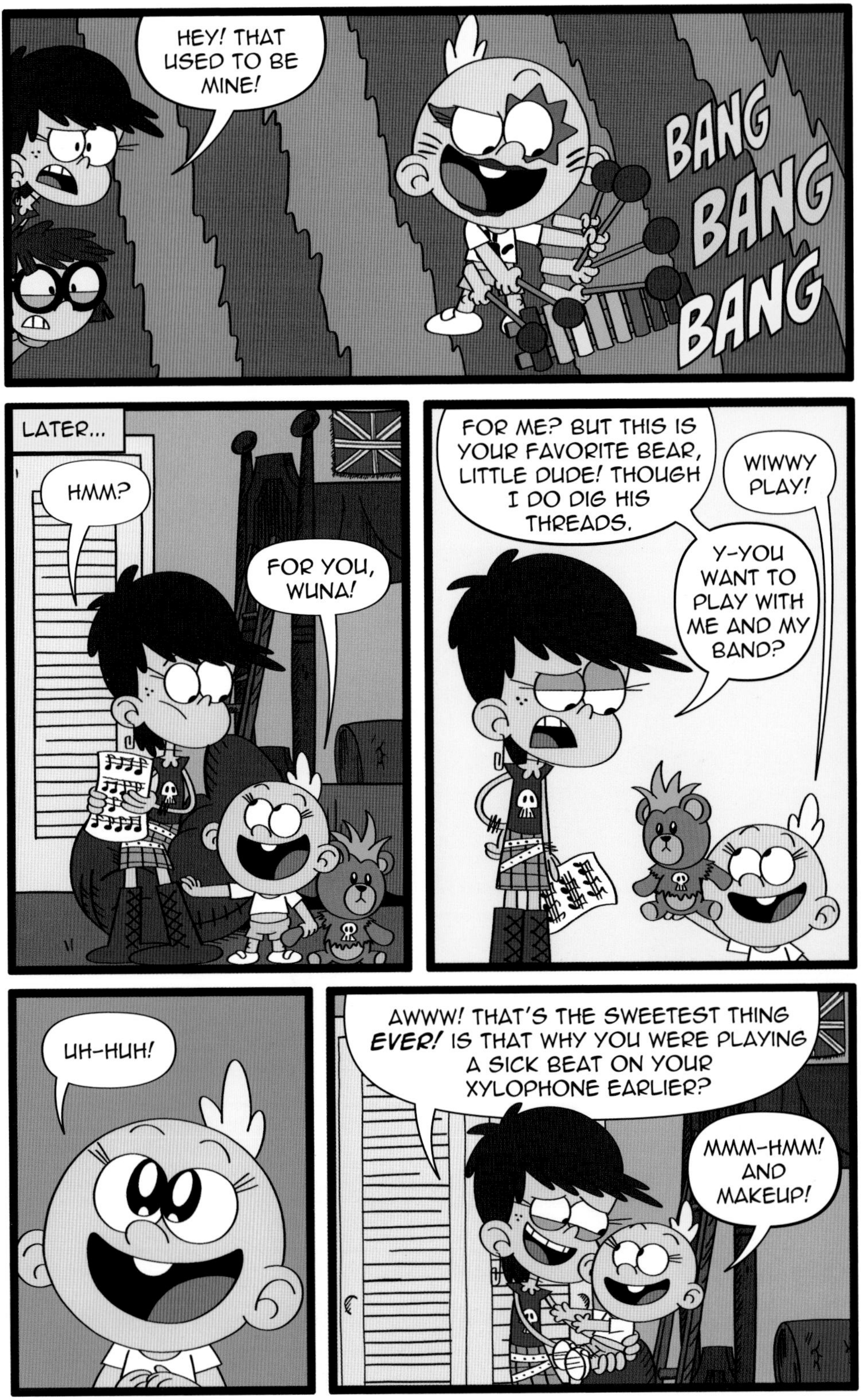
HEY! THAT USED TO BE MINE!
BANG BANG BANG
LATER...
HMM?
FOR YOU, WUNA!
FOR ME? BUT THIS IS YOUR FAVORITE BEAR, LITTLE DUDE! THOUGH I DO DIG HIS THREADS.
WIWWY PLAY!
Y-YOU WANT TO PLAY WITH ME AND MY BAND?
UH-HUH!
AWWW! THAT'S THE SWEETEST THING EVER! IS THAT WHY YOU WERE PLAYING A SICK BEAT ON YOUR XYLOPHONE EARLIER?
MMM-HMM! AND MAKEUP!

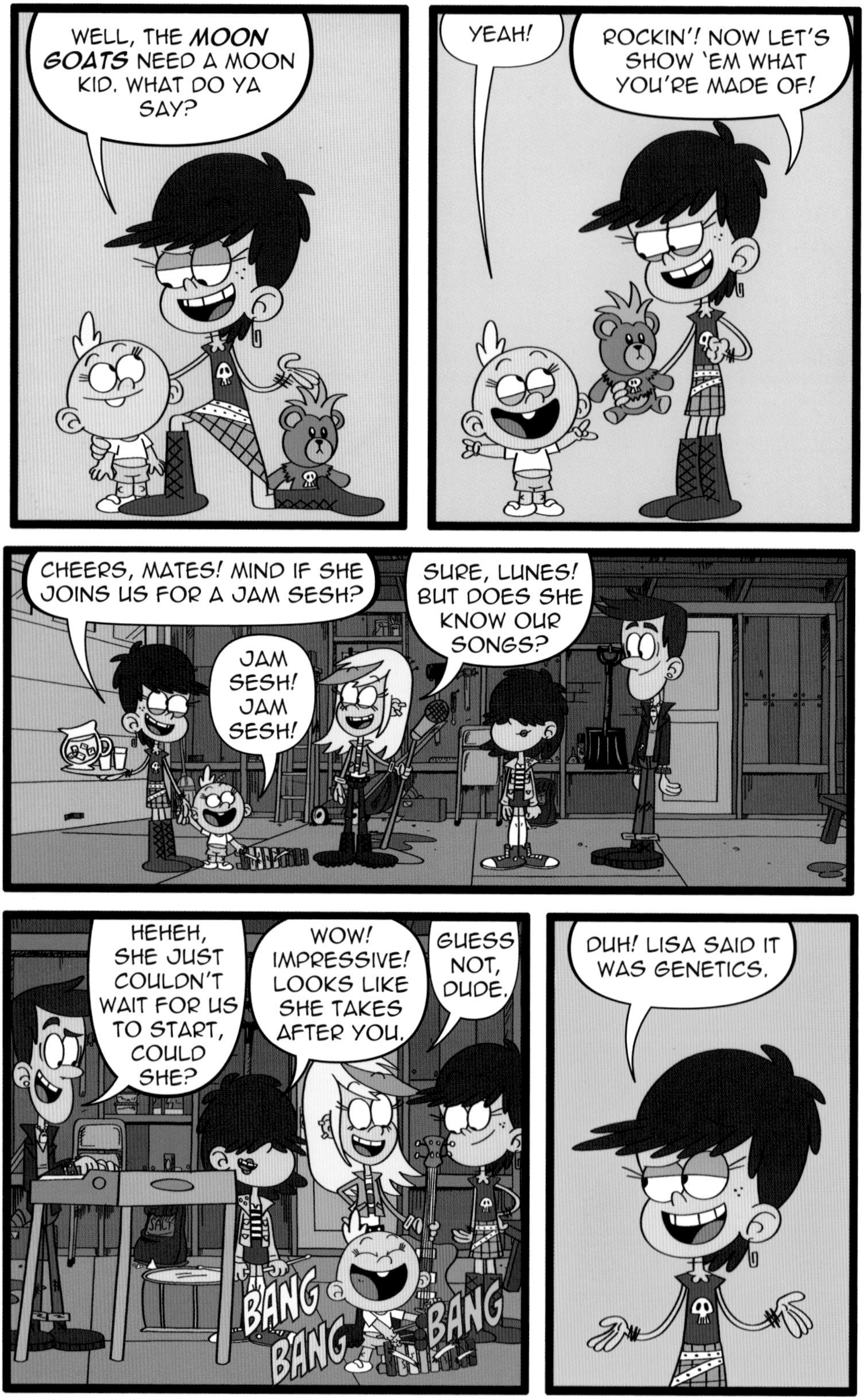
WELL, THE MOON GOATS NEED A MOON KID. WHAT DO YA SAY?
YEAH!
ROCKIN'! NOW LET'S SHOW 'EM WHAT YOU'RE MADE OF!
CHEERS, MATES! MIND IF SHE JOINS US FOR A JAM SESH?
JAM SESH! JAM SESH!
SURE, LUNES! BUT DOES SHE KNOW OUR SONGS?
HEHEH, SHE JUST COULDN'T WAIT FOR US TO START, COULD SHE?
WOW! IMPRESSIVE! LOOKS LIKE SHE TAKES AFTER YOU.
GUESS NOT, DUDE.
BANG
BANG
BANG
DUH! LISA SAID IT WAS GENETICS.

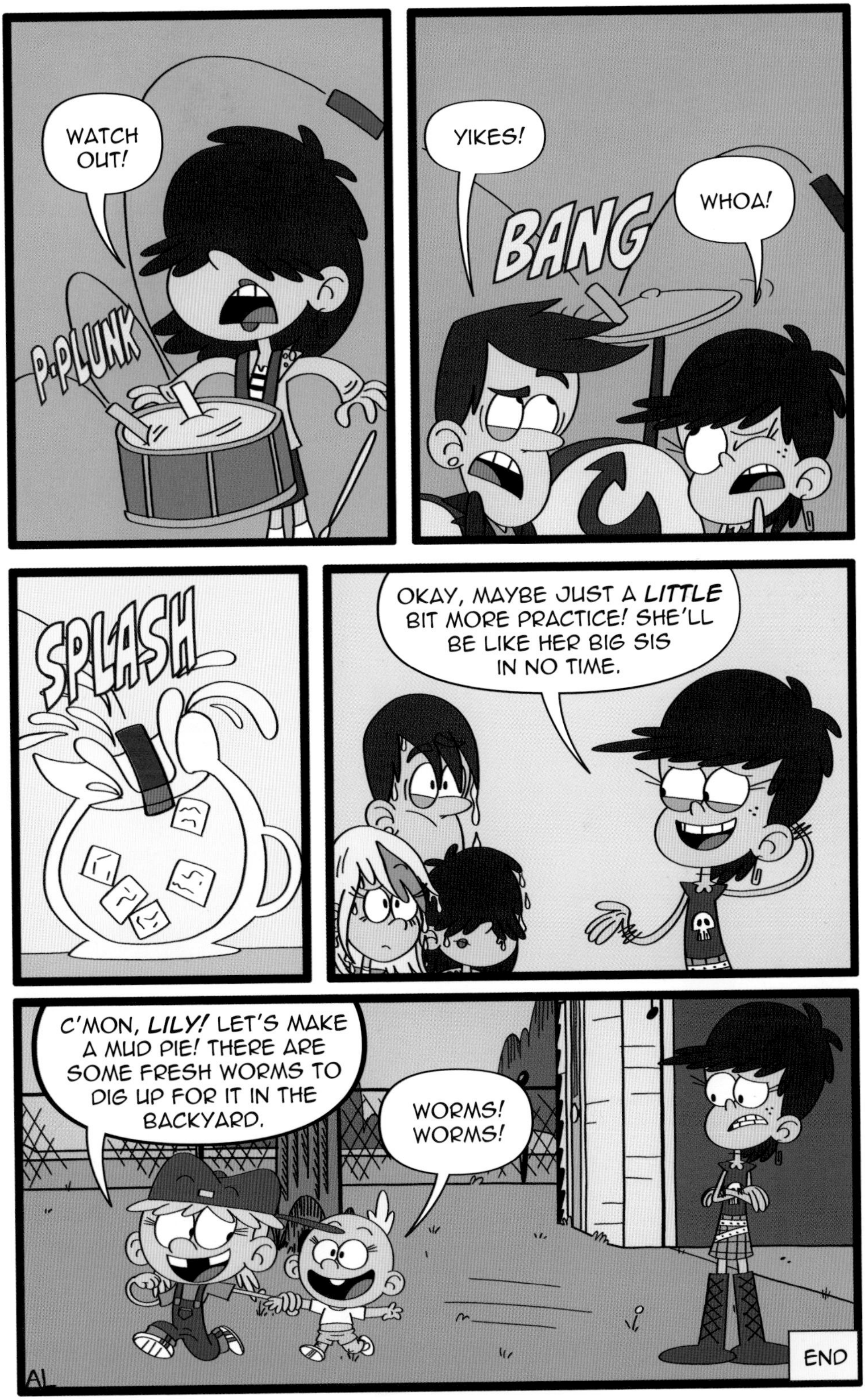
WATCH OUT!
P-PLUNK
YIKES!
BANG
WHOA!
SPLASH
OKAY, MAYBE JUST A *LITTLE* BIT MORE PRACTICE! SHE'LL BE LIKE HER BIG SIS IN NO TIME.
C'MON, *LILY!* LET'S MAKE A MUD PIE! THERE ARE SOME FRESH WORMS TO DIG UP FOR IT IN THE BACKYARD.
WORMS! WORMS!
END
AL

"HAZARDOUS CONDITIONS"

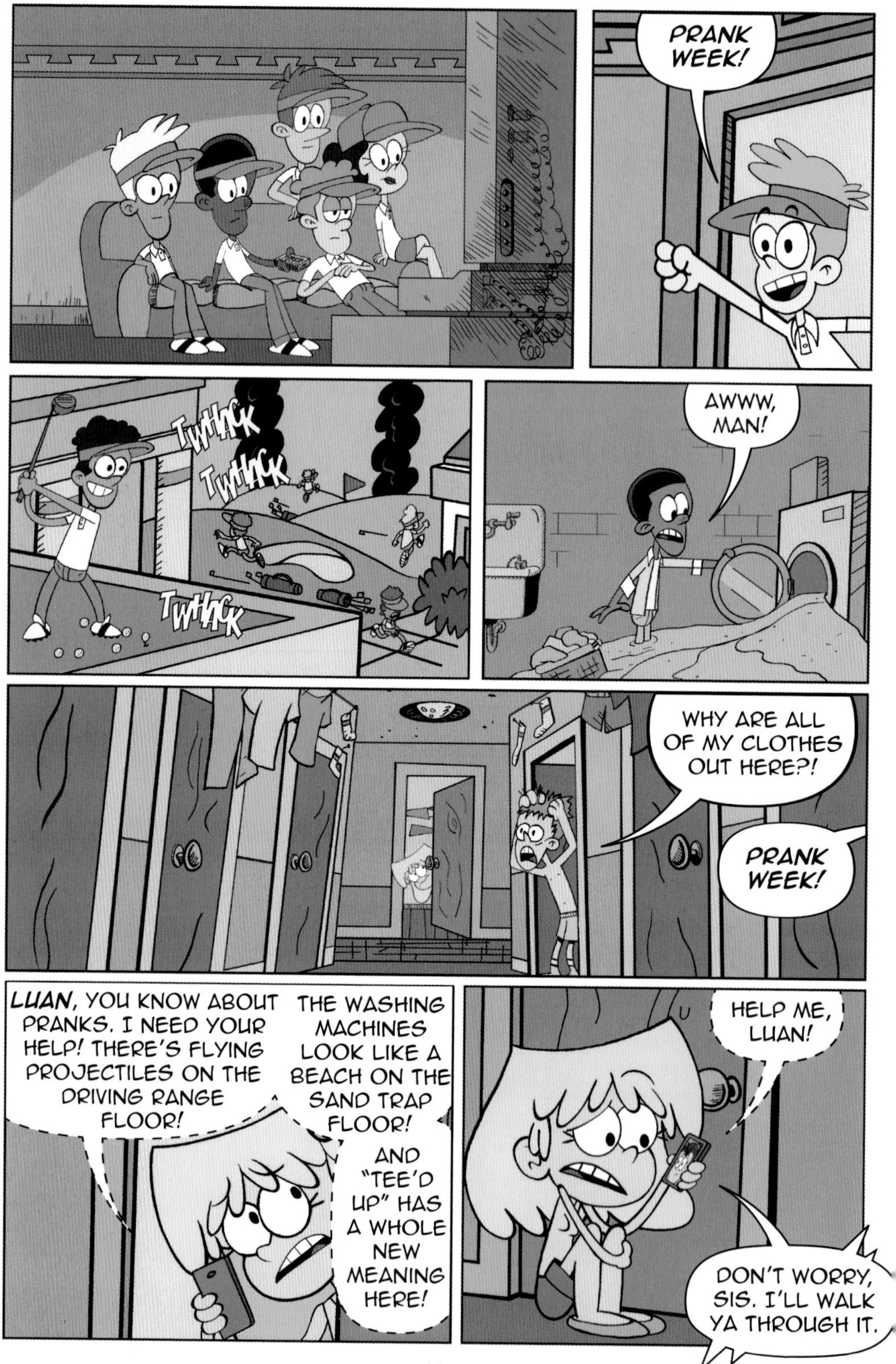
PRANK WEEK!
TWHACK
TWHACK
TWHACK
AWWW, MAN!
WHY ARE ALL OF MY CLOTHES OUT HERE?!
PRANK WEEK!
LUAN, YOU KNOW ABOUT PRANKS. I NEED YOUR HELP! THERE'S FLYING PROJECTILES ON THE DRIVING RANGE FLOOR!
THE WASHING MACHINES LOOK LIKE A BEACH ON THE SAND TRAP FLOOR!
AND "TEE'D UP" HAS A WHOLE NEW MEANING HERE!
HELP ME, LUAN!
DON'T WORRY, SIS. I'LL WALK YA THROUGH IT.

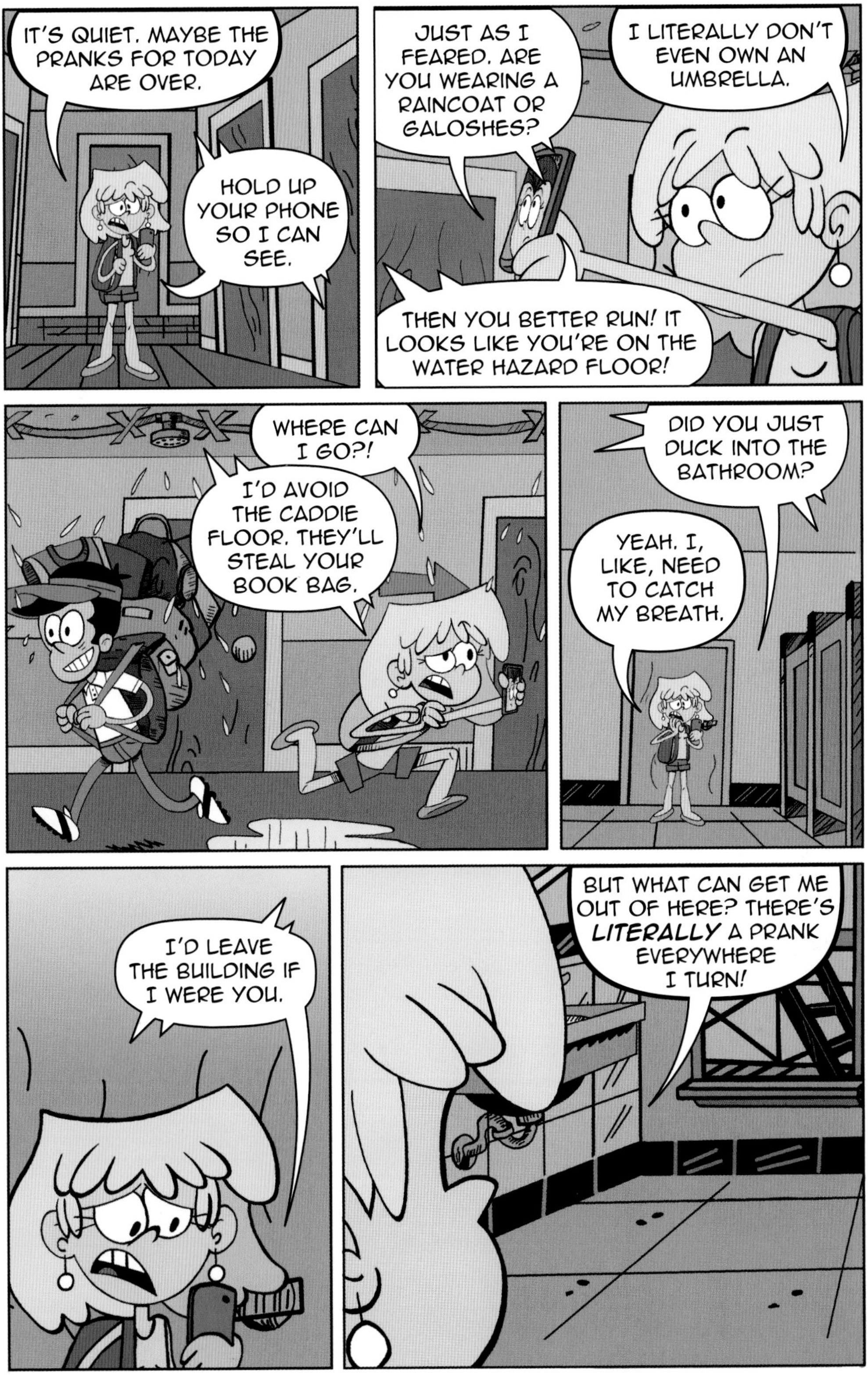
IT'S QUIET. MAYBE THE PRANKS FOR TODAY ARE OVER.
HOLD UP YOUR PHONE SO I CAN SEE.
JUST AS I FEARED. ARE YOU WEARING A RAINCOAT OR GALOSHES?
I LITERALLY DON'T EVEN OWN AN UMBRELLA.
THEN YOU BETTER RUN! IT LOOKS LIKE YOU'RE ON THE WATER HAZARD FLOOR!
WHERE CAN I GO?!
I'D AVOID THE CADDIE FLOOR. THEY'LL STEAL YOUR BOOK BAG.
DID YOU JUST DUCK INTO THE BATHROOM?
YEAH. I, LIKE, NEED TO CATCH MY BREATH.
I'D LEAVE THE BUILDING IF I WERE YOU.
BUT WHAT CAN GET ME OUT OF HERE? THERE'S *LITERALLY* A PRANK EVERYWHERE I TURN!

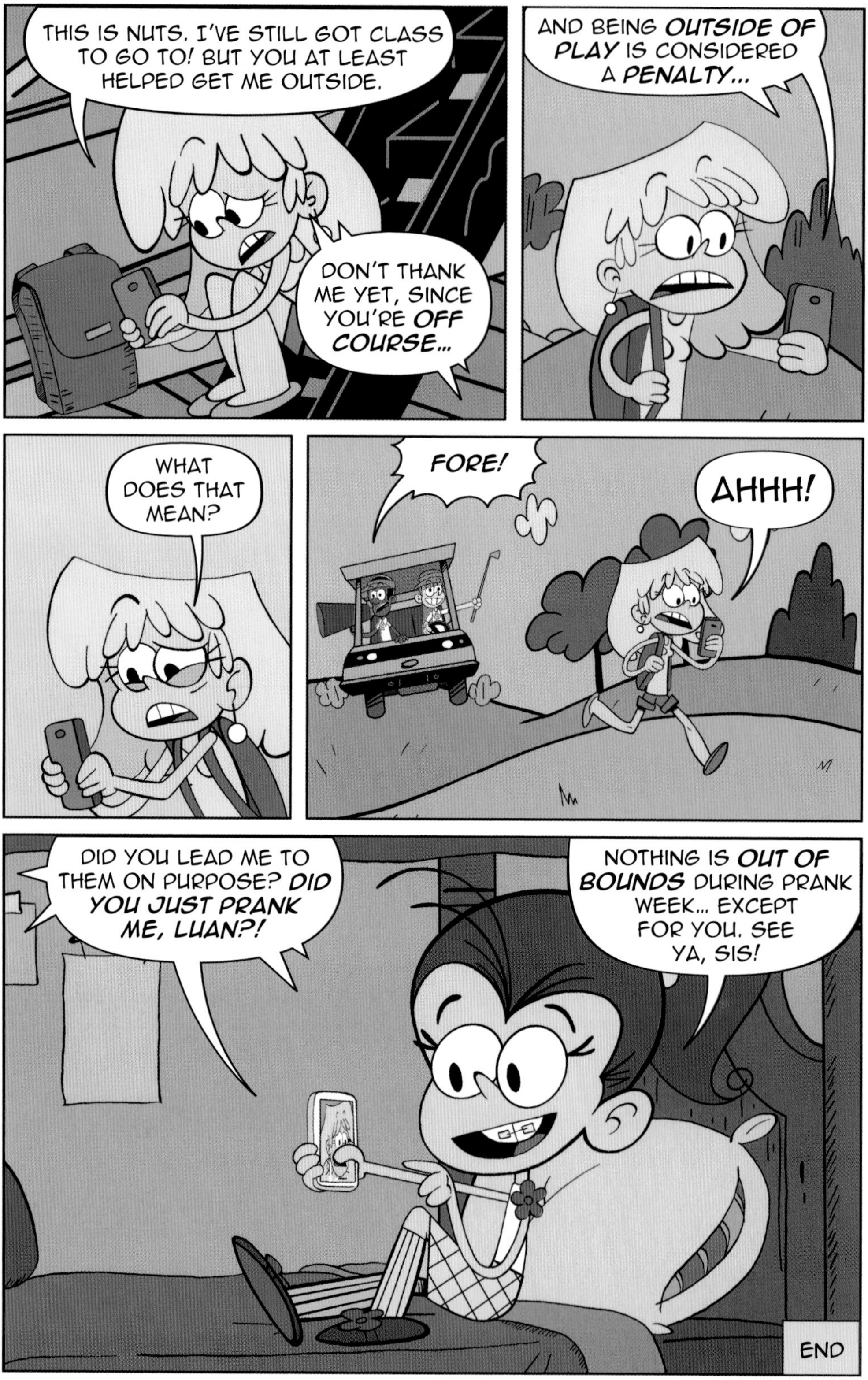
THIS IS NUTS. I'VE STILL GOT CLASS TO GO TO! BUT YOU AT LEAST HELPED GET ME OUTSIDE.
DON'T THANK ME YET, SINCE YOU'RE OFF COURSE...
AND BEING OUTSIDE OF PLAY IS CONSIDERED A PENALTY...
WHAT DOES THAT MEAN?
FORE!
AHHH!
DID YOU LEAD ME TO THEM ON PURPOSE? DID YOU JUST PRANK ME, LUAN?!
NOTHING IS OUT OF BOUNDS DURING PRANK WEEK... EXCEPT FOR YOU. SEE YA, SIS!
END

"FAMILY A CALLING"

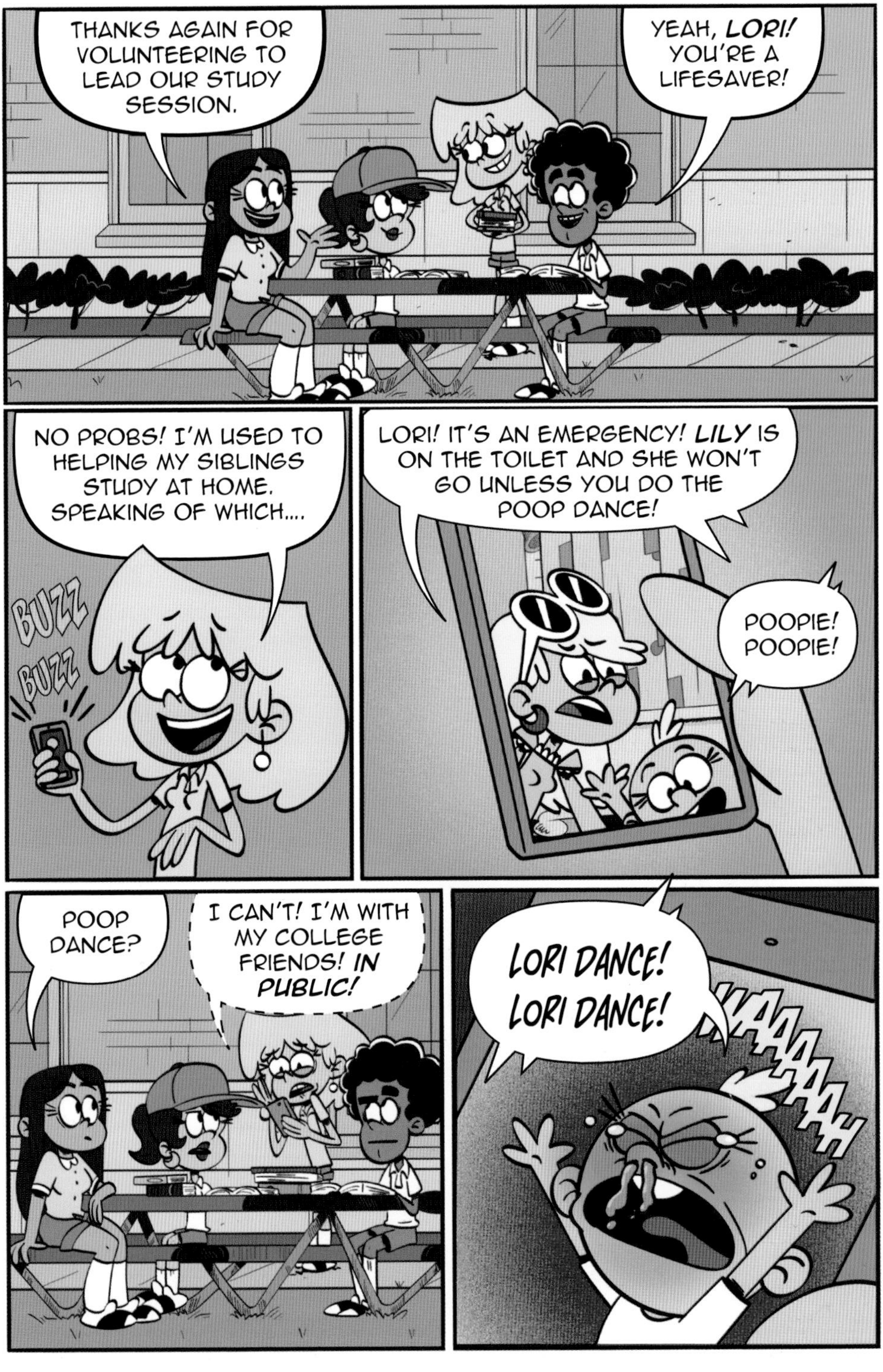
THANKS AGAIN FOR VOLUNTEERING TO LEAD OUR STUDY SESSION.
YEAH, LORI! YOU'RE A LIFESAVER!
NO PROBS! I'M USED TO HELPING MY SIBLINGS STUDY AT HOME. SPEAKING OF WHICH....
BUZZ
BUZZ
LORI! IT'S AN EMERGENCY! LILY IS ON THE TOILET AND SHE WON'T GO UNLESS YOU DO THE POOP DANCE!
POOPIE! POOPIE!
POOP DANCE?
I CAN'T! I'M WITH MY COLLEGE FRIENDS! IN PUBLIC!
LORI DANCE! LORI DANCE!
WAAAAAAH

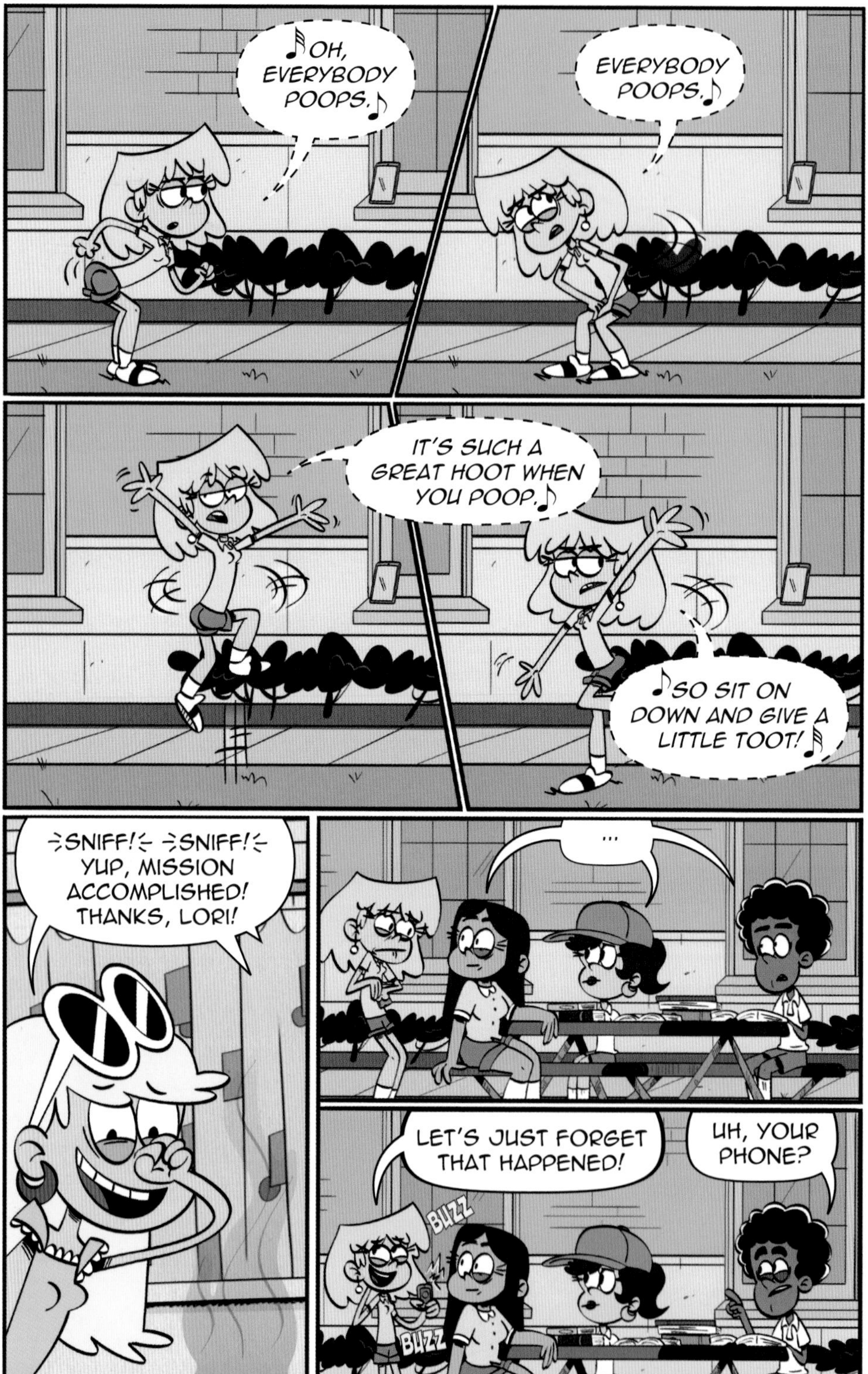

♪OH, EVERYBODY POOPS.♪
EVERYBODY POOPS.♪
IT'S SUCH A GREAT HOOT WHEN YOU POOP.♪
♪SO SIT ON DOWN AND GIVE A LITTLE TOOT!♬
SNIFF! SNIFF! YUP, MISSION ACCOMPLISHED! THANKS, LORI!
...
LET'S JUST FORGET THAT HAPPENED!
UH, YOUR PHONE?
BUZZ
BUZZ

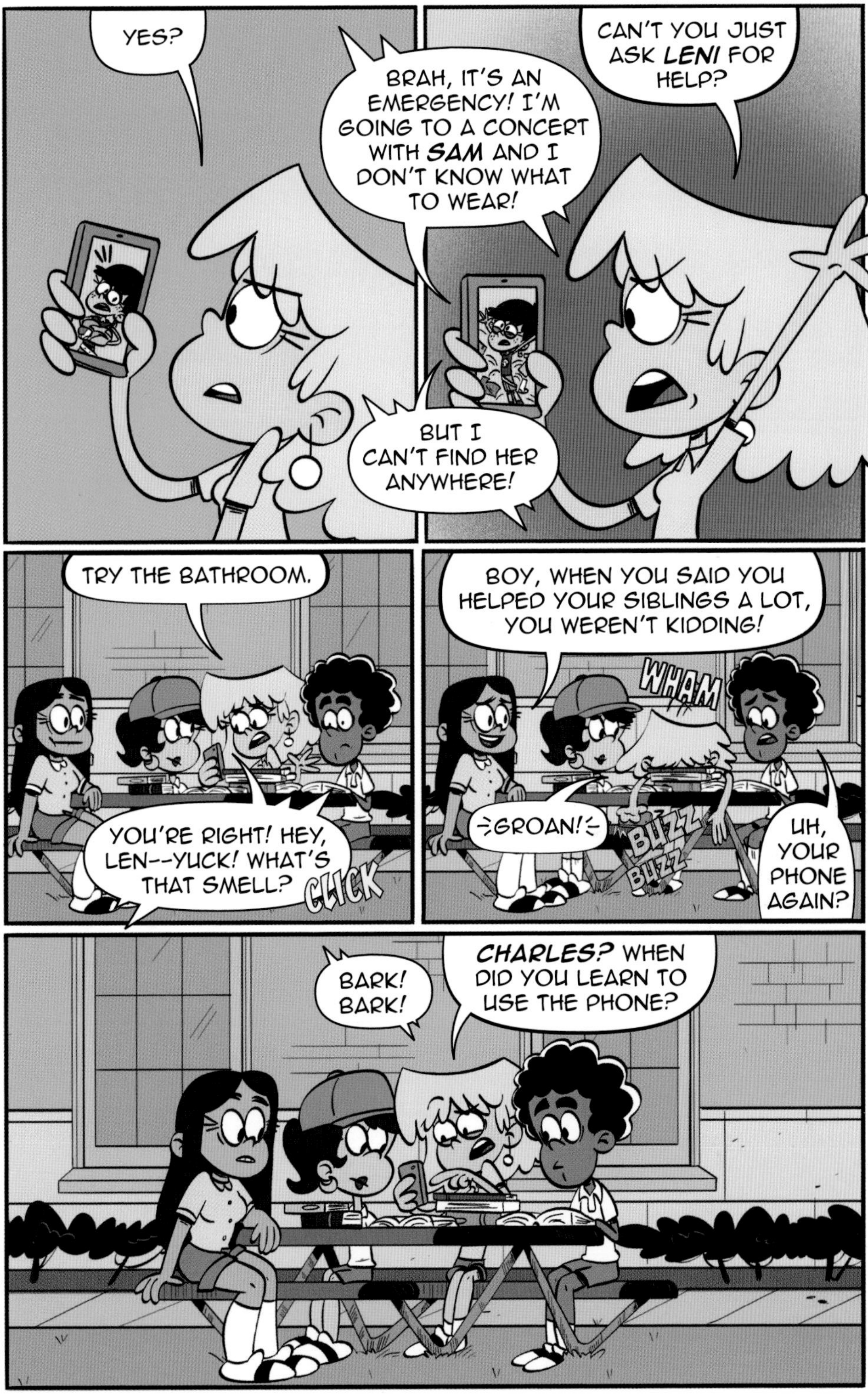

YES?
BRAH, IT'S AN EMERGENCY! I'M GOING TO A CONCERT WITH *SAM* AND I DON'T KNOW WHAT TO WEAR!
CAN'T YOU JUST ASK *LENI* FOR HELP?
BUT I CAN'T FIND HER ANYWHERE!
TRY THE BATHROOM.
YOU'RE RIGHT! HEY, LEN--YUCK! WHAT'S THAT SMELL?
CLICK
BOY, WHEN YOU SAID YOU HELPED YOUR SIBLINGS A LOT, YOU WEREN'T KIDDING!
WHAM
GROAN!
BUZZ BUZZ
UH, YOUR PHONE AGAIN?
BARK! BARK!
CHARLES? WHEN DID YOU LEARN TO USE THE PHONE?

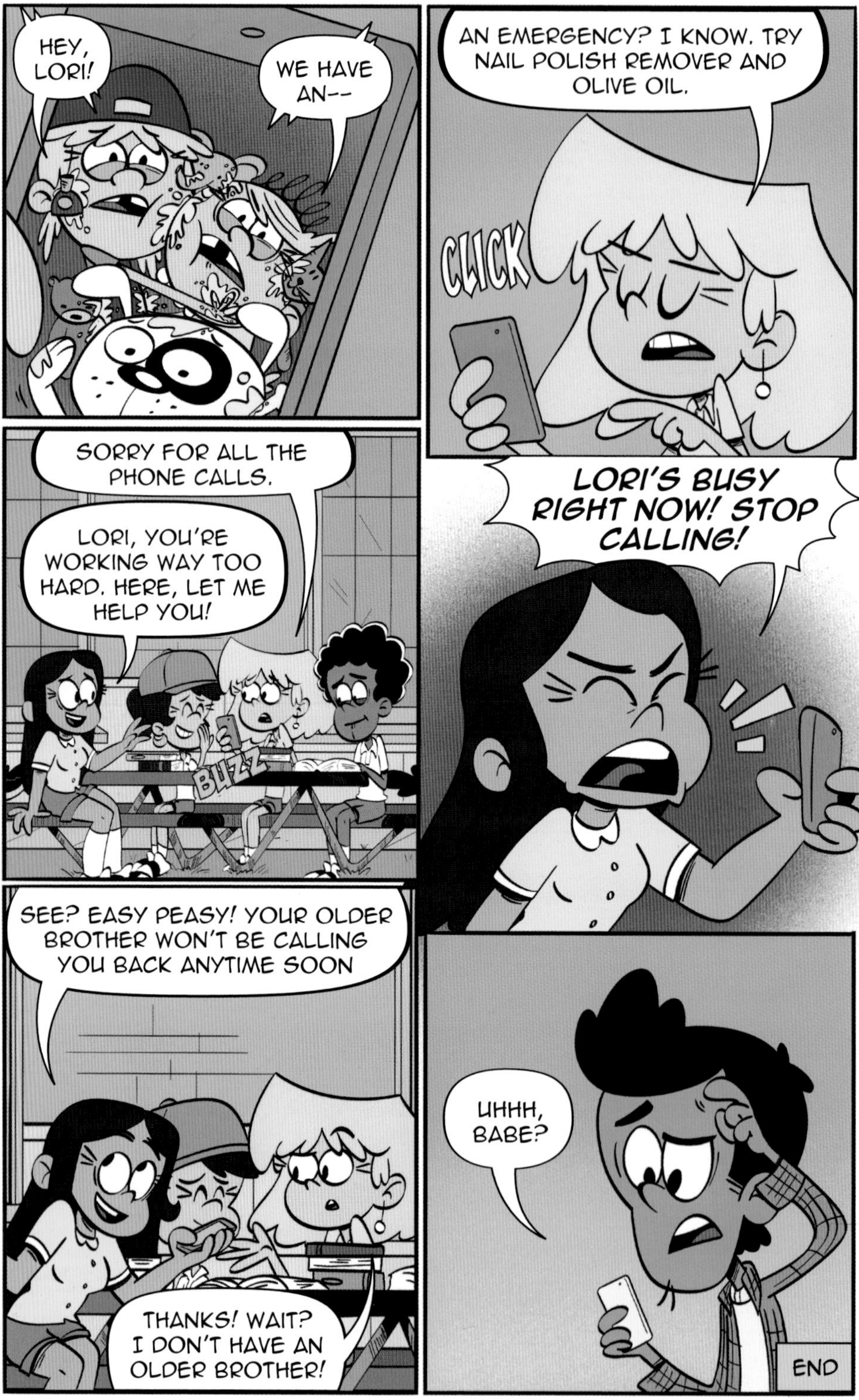
HEY, LORI!
WE HAVE AN--
AN EMERGENCY? I KNOW. TRY NAIL POLISH REMOVER AND OLIVE OIL.
CLICK
SORRY FOR ALL THE PHONE CALLS.
LORI, YOU'RE WORKING WAY TOO HARD. HERE, LET ME HELP YOU!
BUZZ
LORI'S BUSY RIGHT NOW! STOP CALLING!
SEE? EASY PEASY! YOUR OLDER BROTHER WON'T BE CALLING YOU BACK ANYTIME SOON
THANKS! WAIT? I DON'T HAVE AN OLDER BROTHER!
UHHH, BABE?
END

"A NOT SO CLOSE ENCOUNTER"

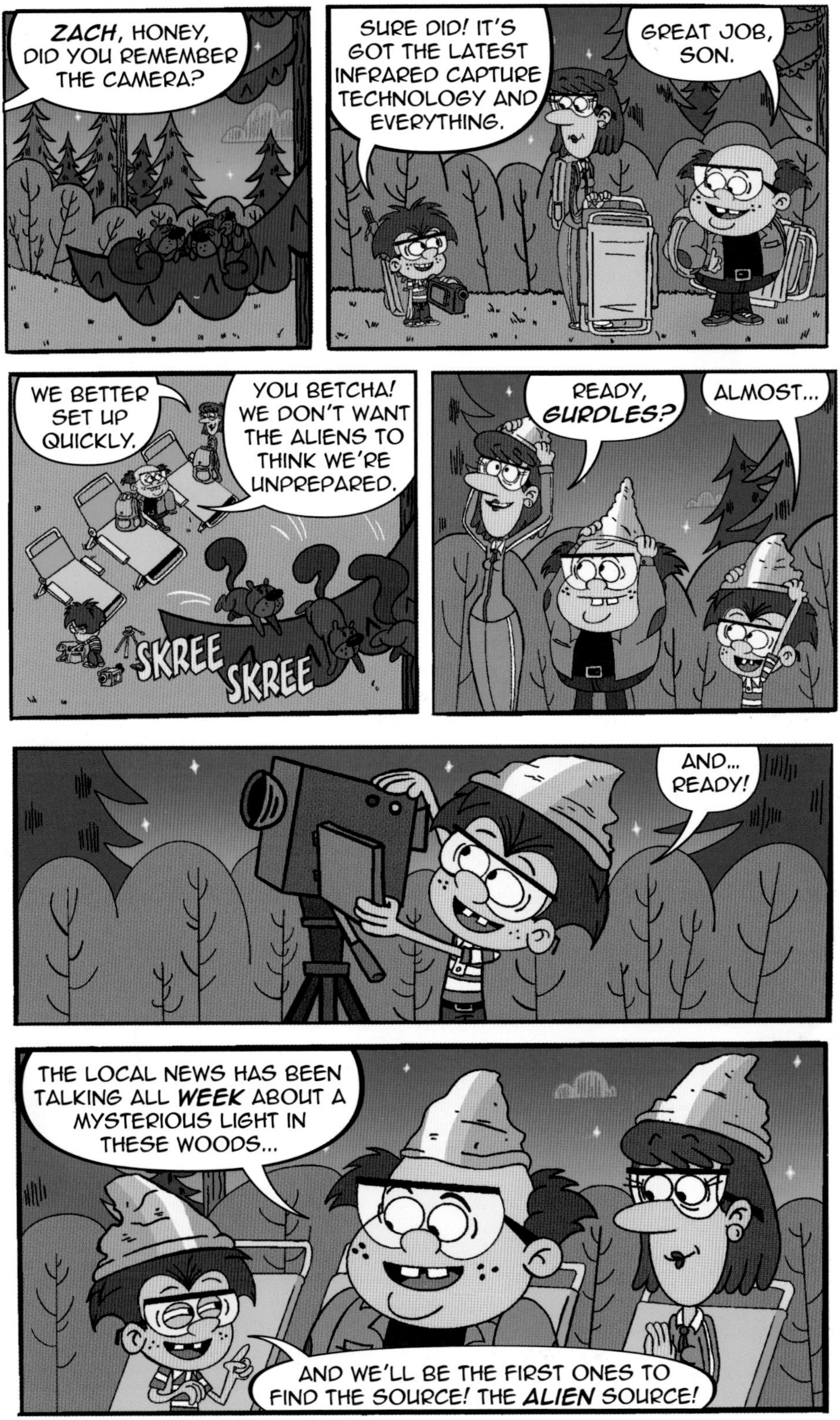
ZACH, HONEY, DID YOU REMEMBER THE CAMERA?
SURE DID! IT'S GOT THE LATEST INFRARED CAPTURE TECHNOLOGY AND EVERYTHING.
GREAT JOB, SON.
WE BETTER SET UP QUICKLY.
YOU BETCHA! WE DON'T WANT THE ALIENS TO THINK WE'RE UNPREPARED.
SKREE
SKREE
READY, GURDLES?
ALMOST...
AND... READY!
THE LOCAL NEWS HAS BEEN TALKING ALL WEEK ABOUT A MYSTERIOUS LIGHT IN THESE WOODS...
AND WE'LL BE THE FIRST ONES TO FIND THE SOURCE! THE ALIEN SOURCE!

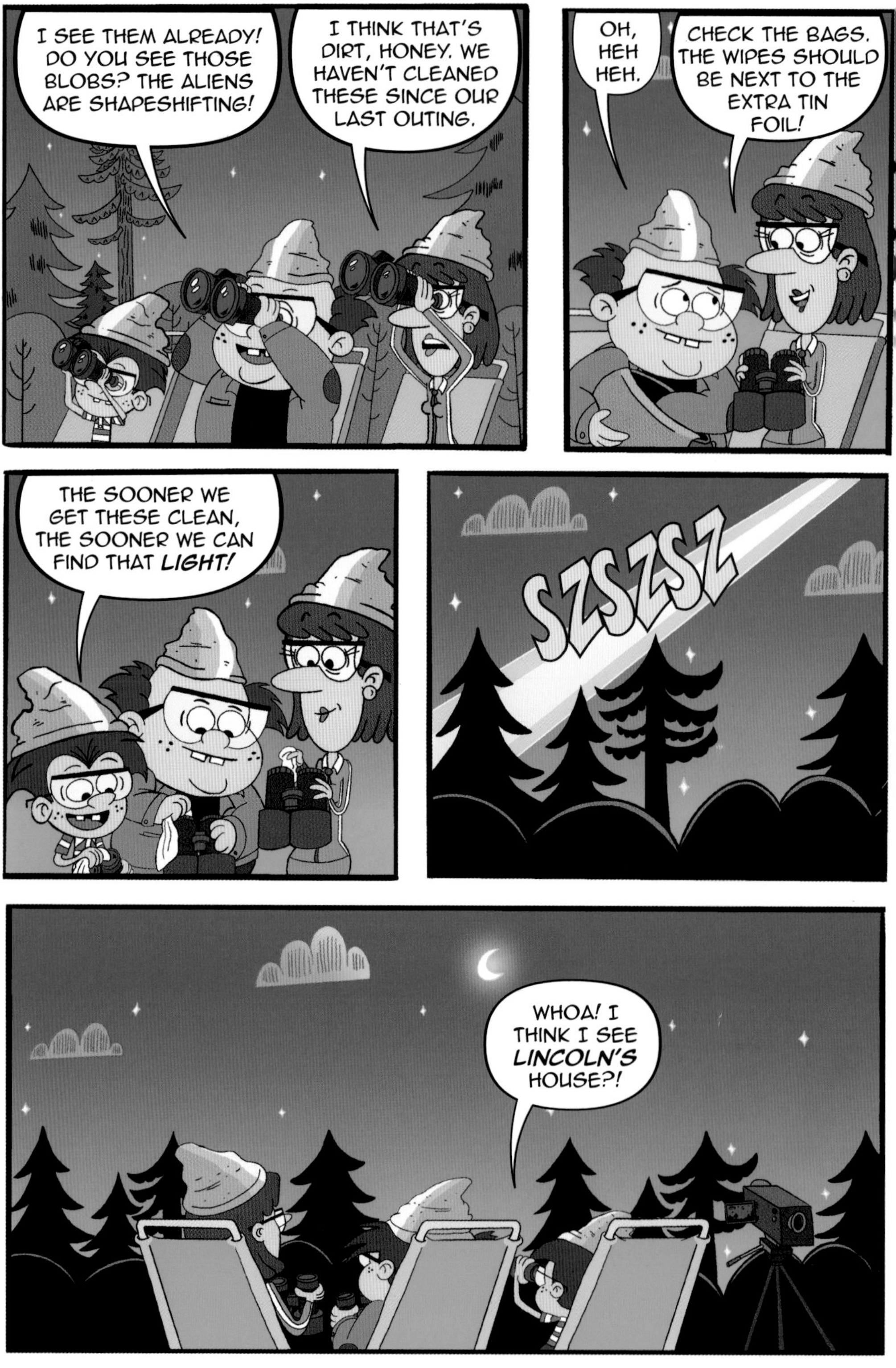
I SEE THEM ALREADY! DO YOU SEE THOSE BLOBS? THE ALIENS ARE SHAPESHIFTING!
I THINK THAT'S DIRT, HONEY. WE HAVEN'T CLEANED THESE SINCE OUR LAST OUTING.
OH, HEH HEH.
CHECK THE BAGS. THE WIPES SHOULD BE NEXT TO THE EXTRA TIN FOIL!
THE SOONER WE GET THESE CLEAN, THE SOONER WE CAN FIND THAT LIGHT!
SZSZSZ
WHOA! I THINK I SEE LINCOLN'S HOUSE?!

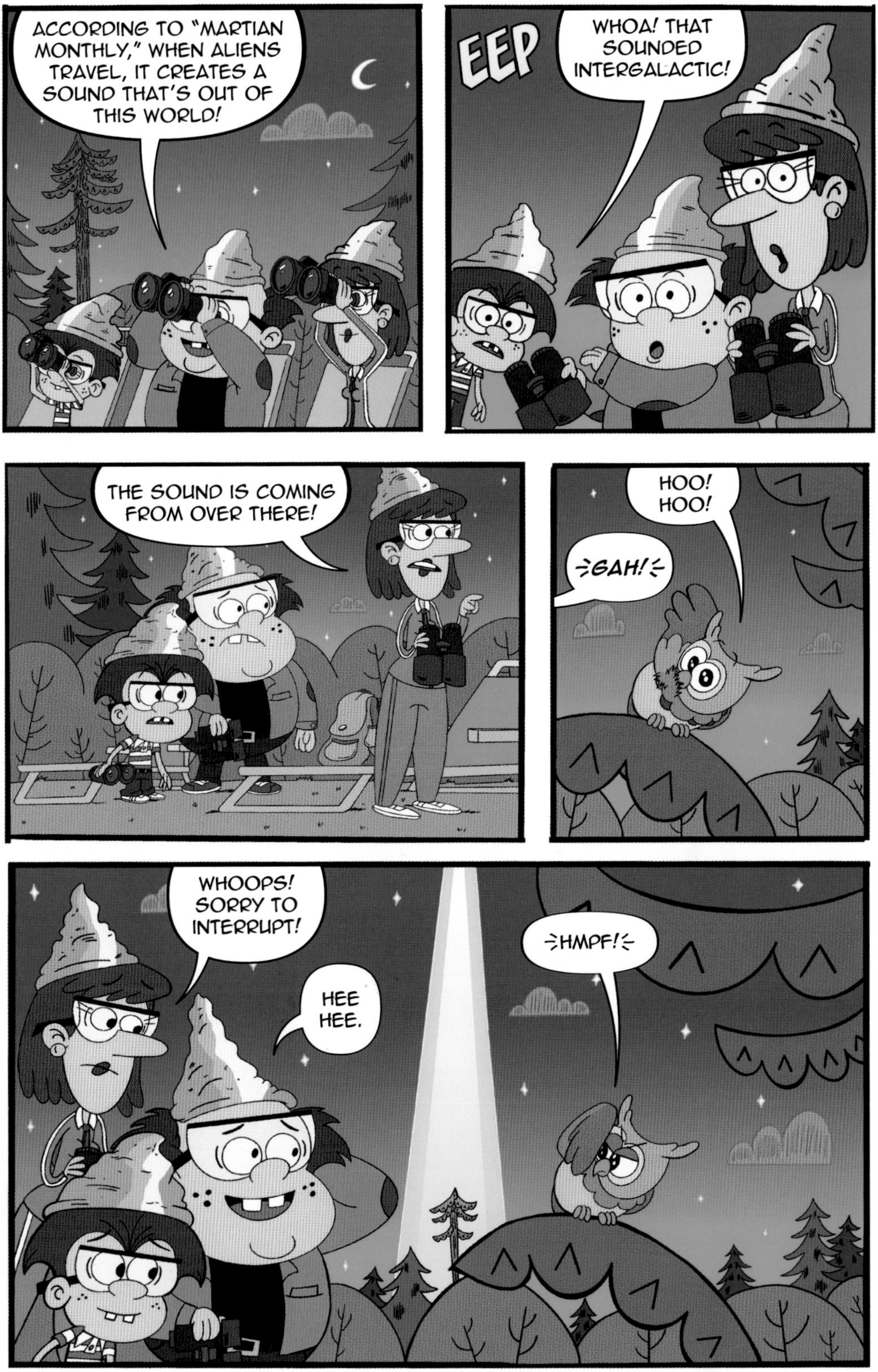
ACCORDING TO "MARTIAN MONTHLY," WHEN ALIENS TRAVEL, IT CREATES A SOUND THAT'S OUT OF THIS WORLD!
EEP
WHOA! THAT SOUNDED INTERGALACTIC!
THE SOUND IS COMING FROM OVER THERE!
HOO! HOO!
GAH!
WHOOPS! SORRY TO INTERRUPT!
HEE HEE.
HMPF!

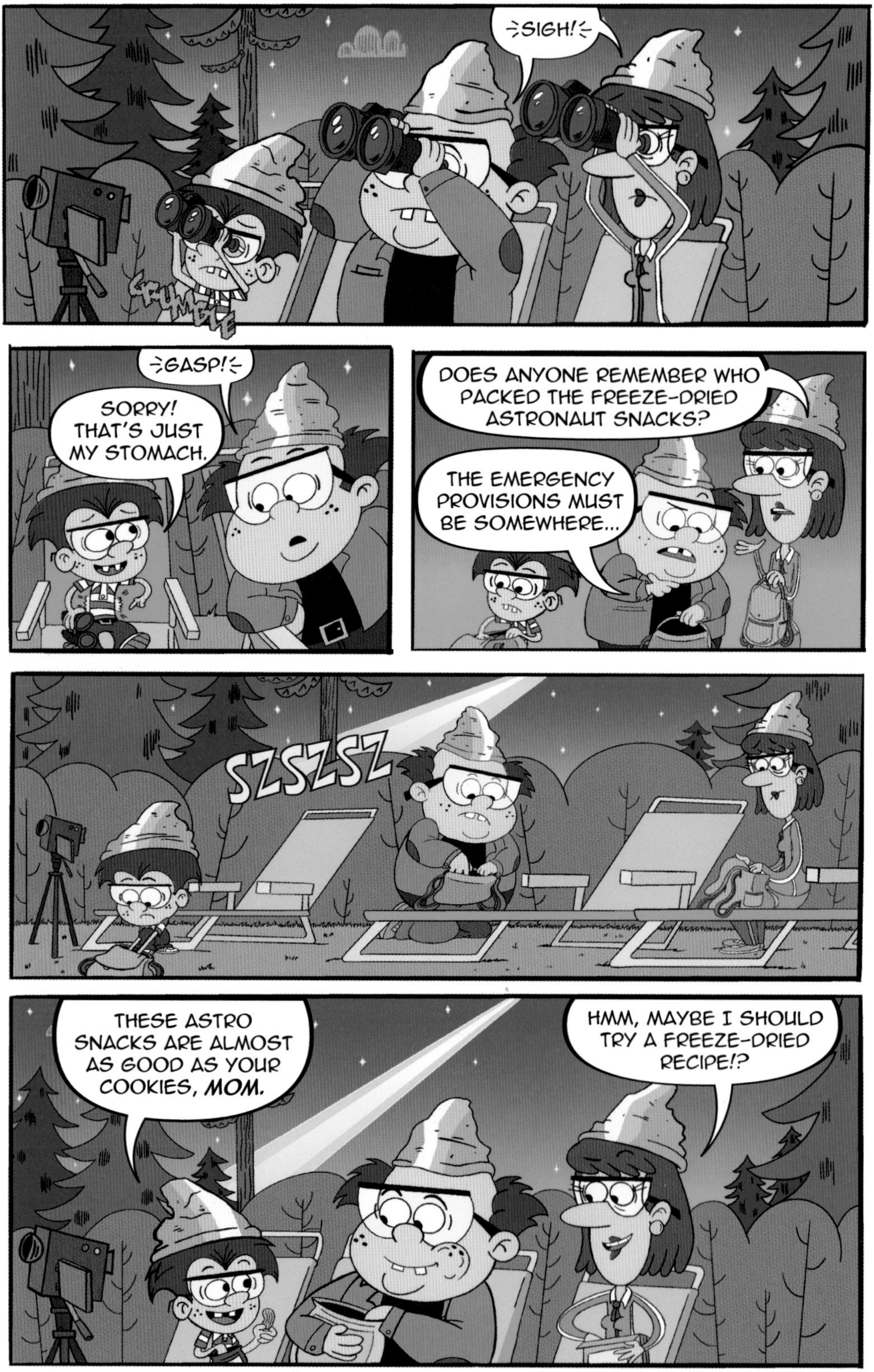

SIGH!
GRUMBLE
GASP!
SORRY! THAT'S JUST MY STOMACH.
DOES ANYONE REMEMBER WHO PACKED THE FREEZE-DRIED ASTRONAUT SNACKS?
THE EMERGENCY PROVISIONS MUST BE SOMEWHERE...
SZSZSZ
THESE ASTRO SNACKS ARE ALMOST AS GOOD AS YOUR COOKIES, MOM.
HMM, MAYBE I SHOULD TRY A FREEZE-DRIED RECIPE!?

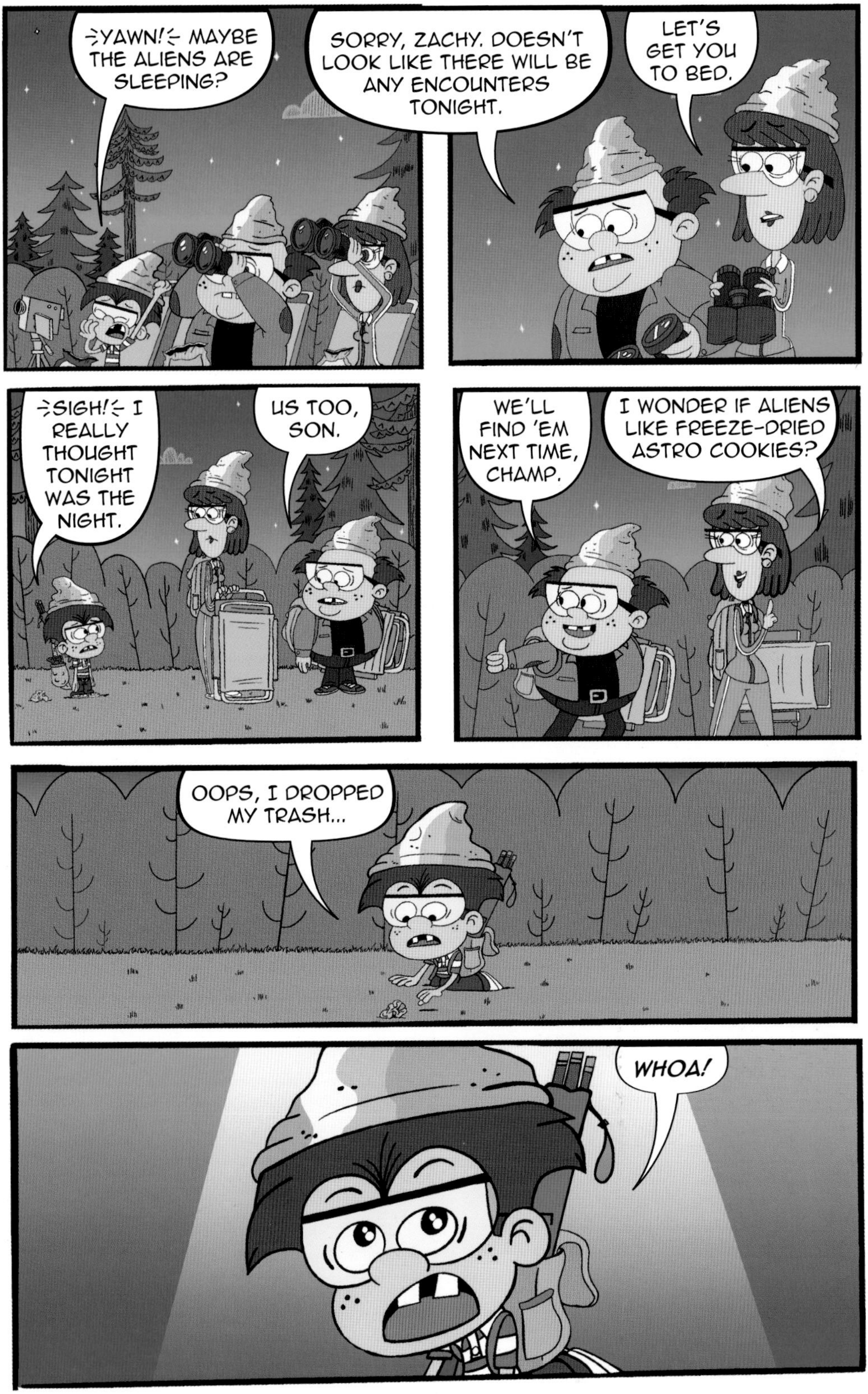
⇒YAWN!⇐ MAYBE THE ALIENS ARE SLEEPING?
SORRY, ZACHY. DOESN'T LOOK LIKE THERE WILL BE ANY ENCOUNTERS TONIGHT.
LET'S GET YOU TO BED.
⇒SIGH!⇐ I REALLY THOUGHT TONIGHT WAS THE NIGHT.
US TOO, SON.
WE'LL FIND 'EM NEXT TIME, CHAMP.
I WONDER IF ALIENS LIKE FREEZE-DRIED ASTRO COOKIES?
OOPS, I DROPPED MY TRASH...
WHOA!

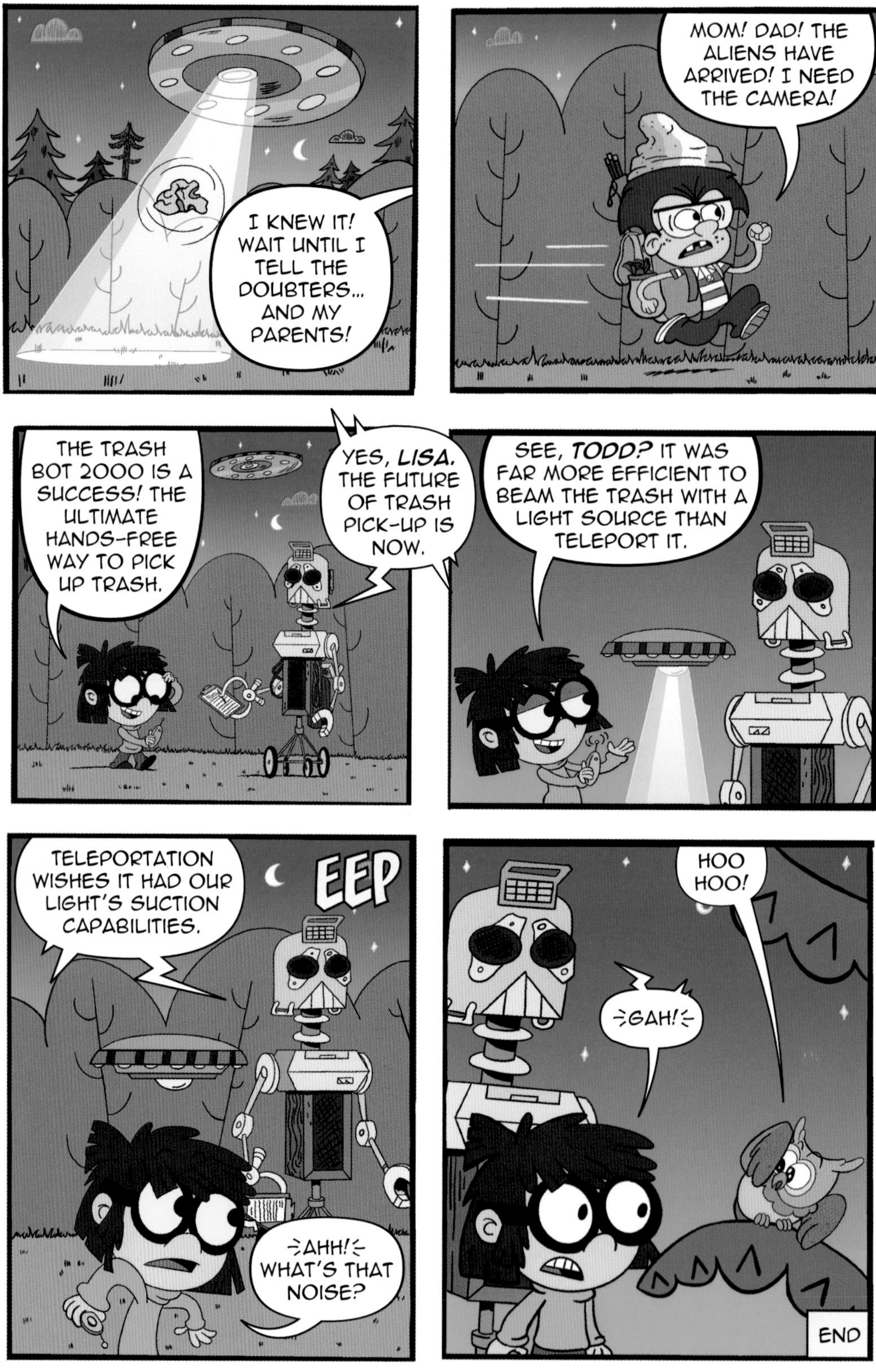
I KNEW IT! WAIT UNTIL I TELL THE DOUBTERS... AND MY PARENTS!
MOM! DAD! THE ALIENS HAVE ARRIVED! I NEED THE CAMERA!
THE TRASH BOT 2000 IS A SUCCESS! THE ULTIMATE HANDS-FREE WAY TO PICK UP TRASH.
YES, LISA. THE FUTURE OF TRASH PICK-UP IS NOW.
SEE, TODD? IT WAS FAR MORE EFFICIENT TO BEAM THE TRASH WITH A LIGHT SOURCE THAN TELEPORT IT.
TELEPORTATION WISHES IT HAD OUR LIGHT'S SUCTION CAPABILITIES.
EEP
AHH! WHAT'S THAT NOISE?
HOO HOO!
GAH!
END

"A PETTY PLAYDATE"

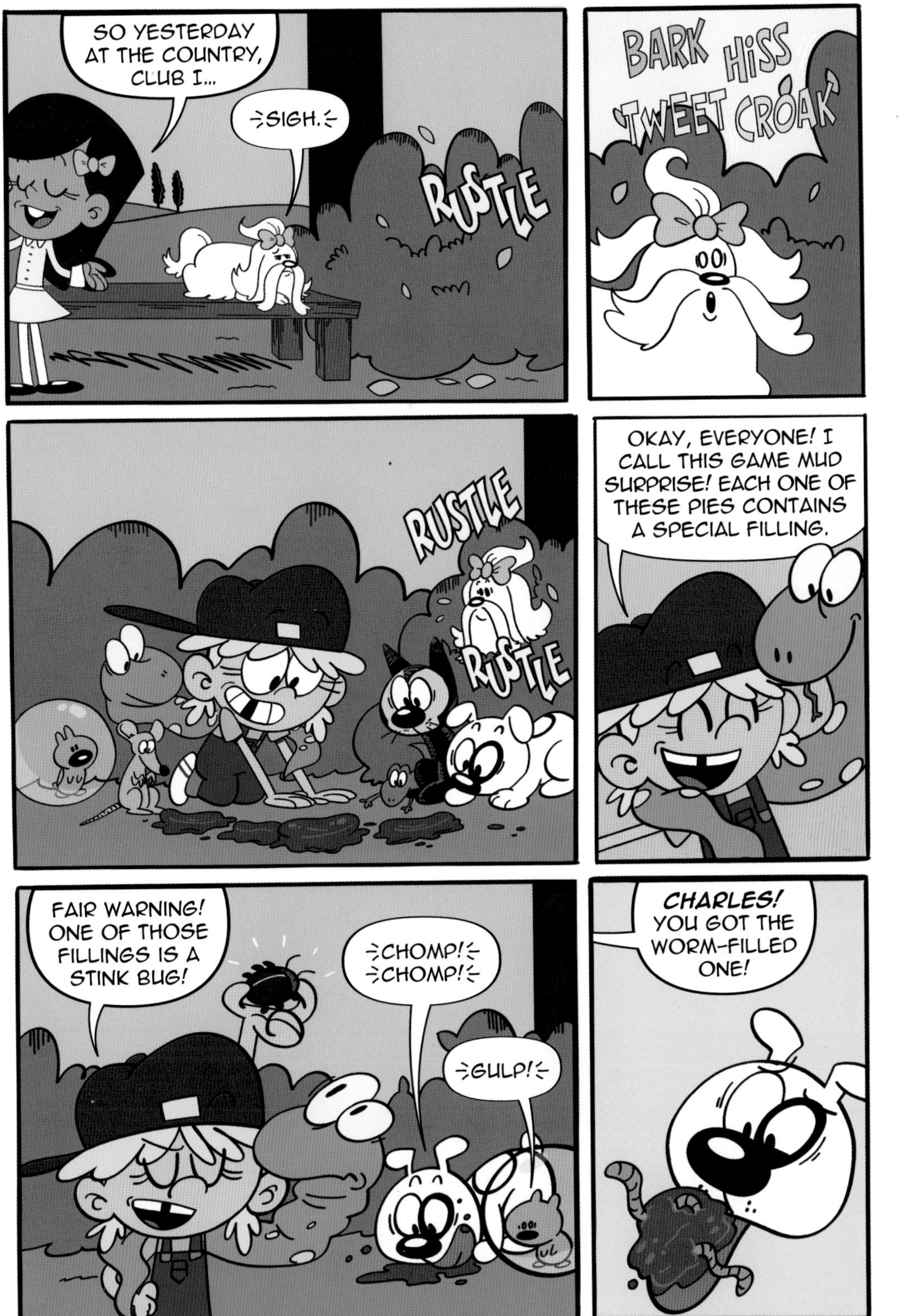
SO YESTERDAY AT THE COUNTRY, CLUB I...
SIGH.
RUSTLE
BARK HISS
TWEET CROAK
RUSTLE
RUSTLE
OKAY, EVERYONE! I CALL THIS GAME MUD SURPRISE! EACH ONE OF THESE PIES CONTAINS A SPECIAL FILLING.
FAIR WARNING! ONE OF THOSE FILLINGS IS A STINK BUG!
CHOMP! CHOMP!
GULP!
CHARLES! YOU GOT THE WORM-FILLED ONE!

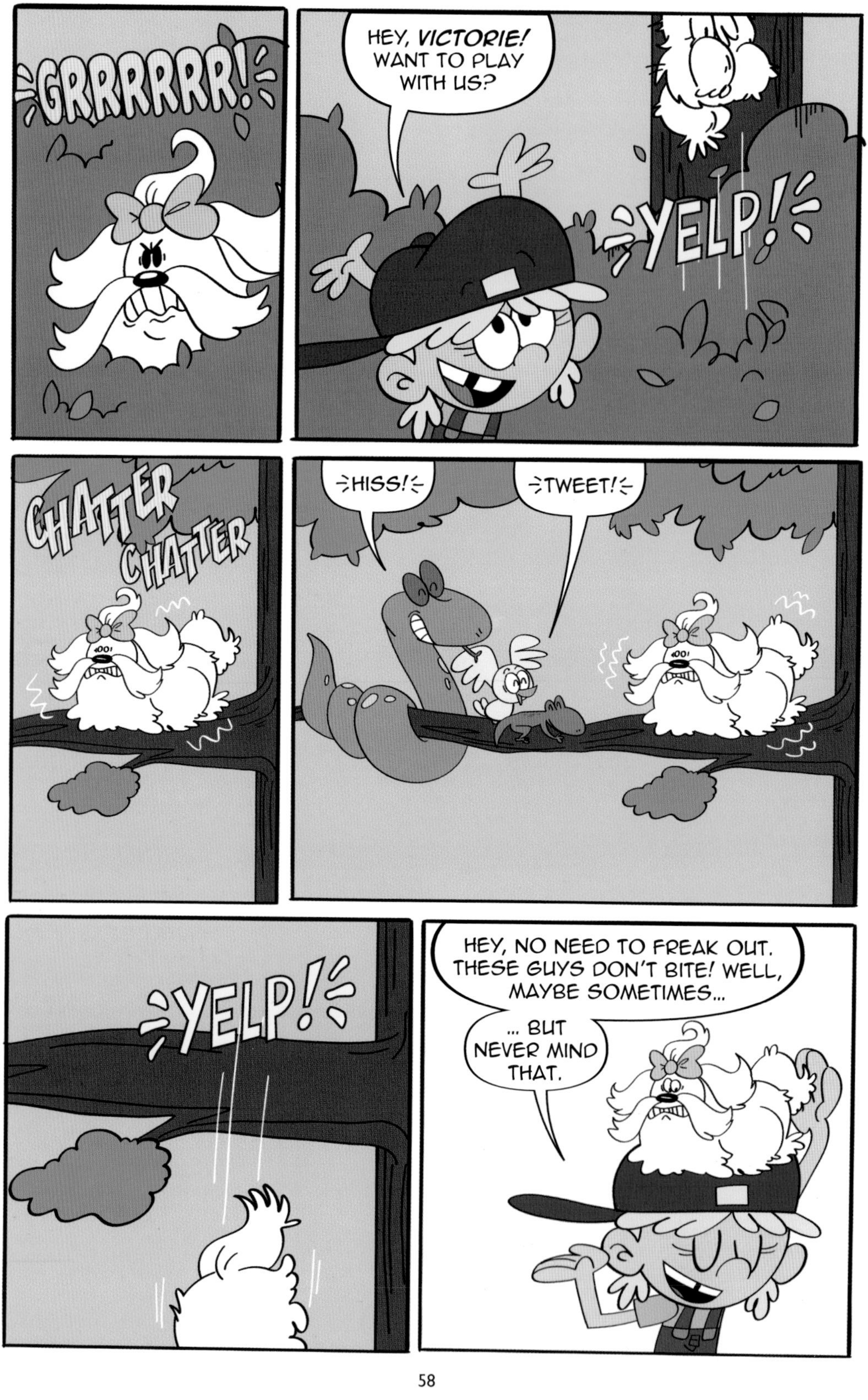
GRRRRRR!
HEY, VICTORIE! WANT TO PLAY WITH US?
YELP!
CHATTER
CHATTER
HISS!
TWEET!
YELP!
HEY, NO NEED TO FREAK OUT. THESE GUYS DON'T BITE! WELL, MAYBE SOMETIMES...
... BUT NEVER MIND THAT.

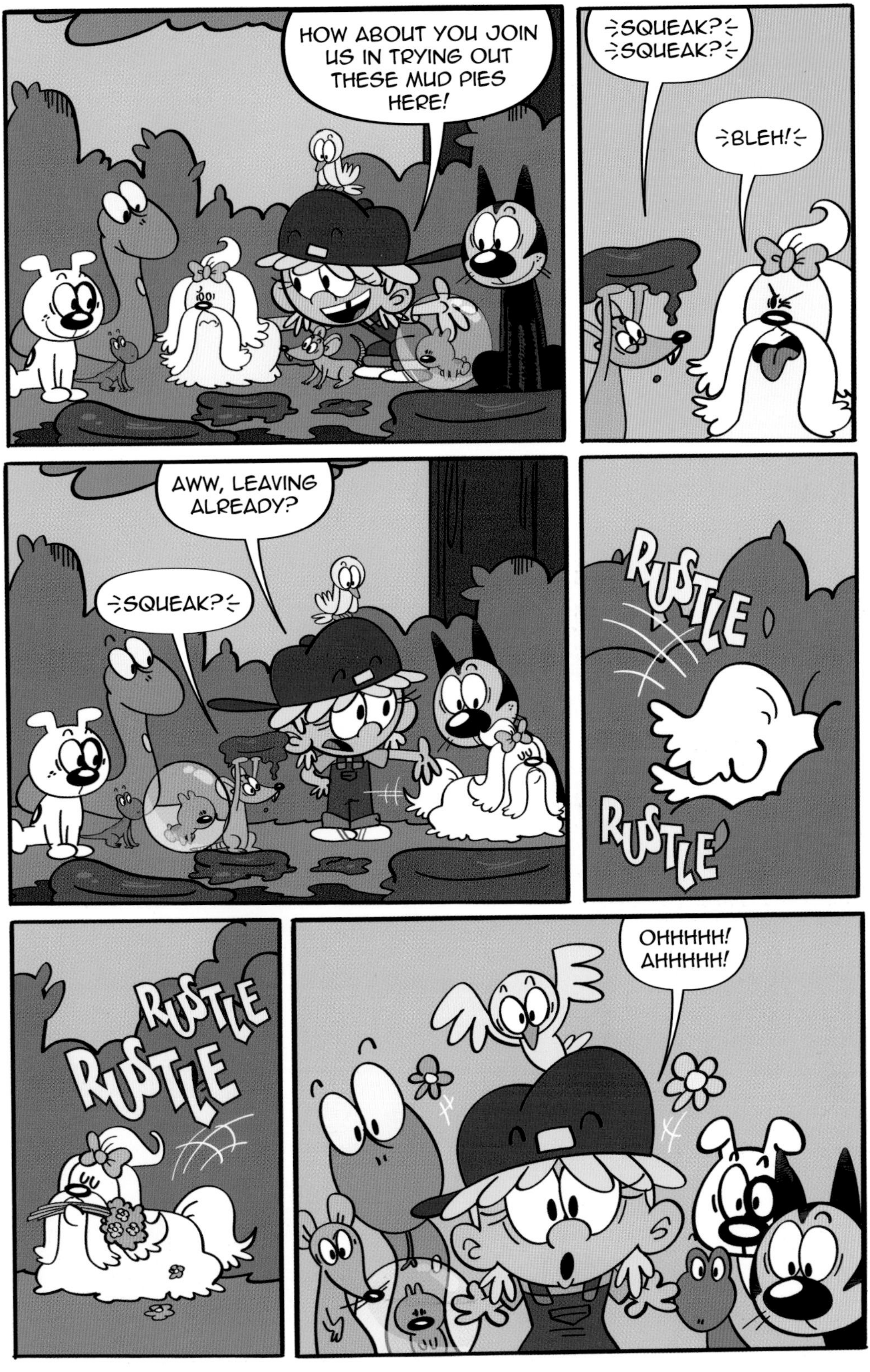
HOW ABOUT YOU JOIN US IN TRYING OUT THESE MUD PIES HERE!
SQUEAK? SQUEAK?
BLEH!
AWW, LEAVING ALREADY?
SQUEAK?
RUSTLE
RUSTLE
RUSTLE
RUSTLE
OHHHHH! AHHHHH!

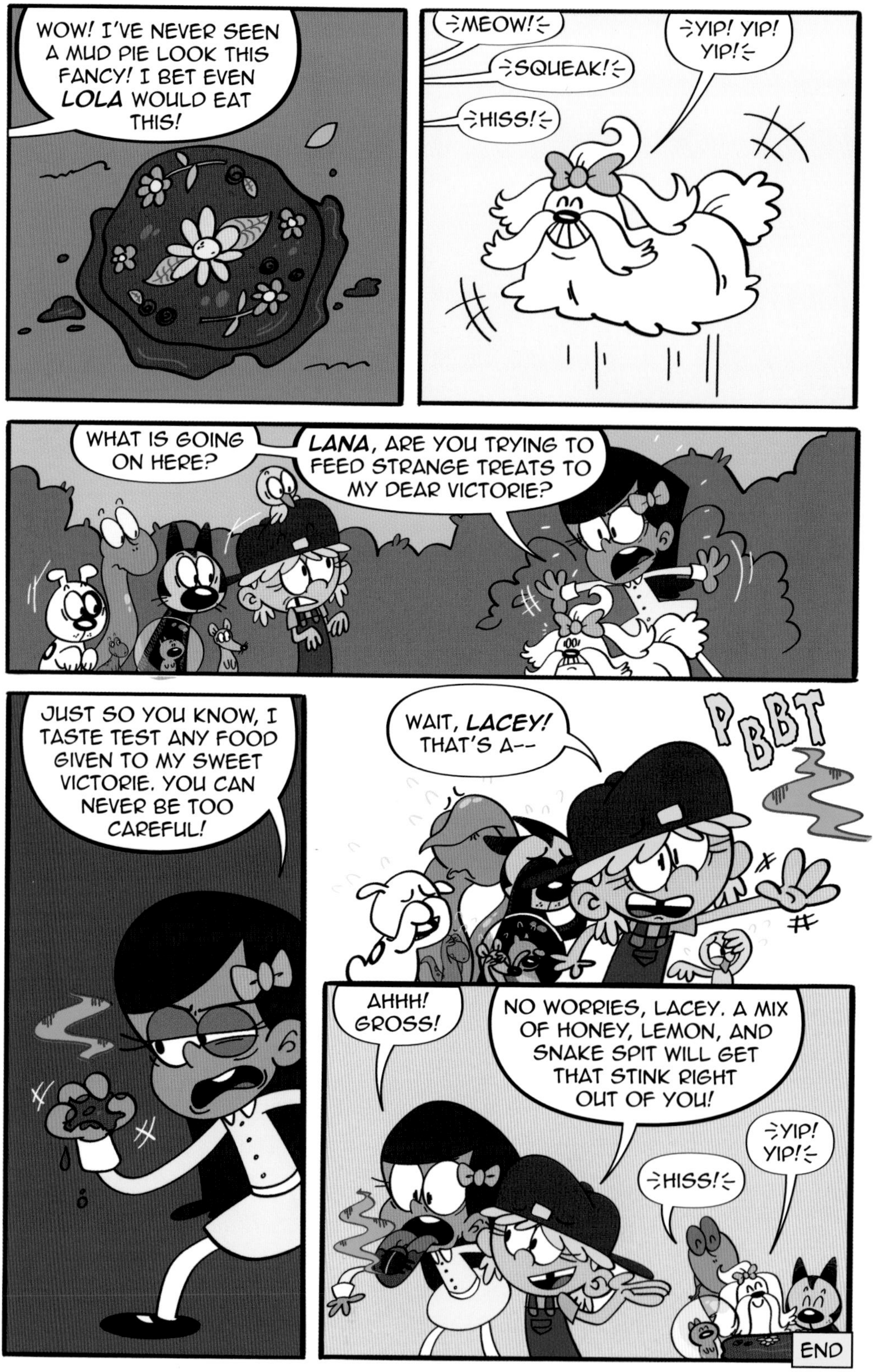
WOW! I'VE NEVER SEEN A MUD PIE LOOK THIS FANCY! I BET EVEN LOLA WOULD EAT THIS!
MEOW!
SQUEAK!
HISS!
YIP! YIP! YIP!
WHAT IS GOING ON HERE?
LANA, ARE YOU TRYING TO FEED STRANGE TREATS TO MY DEAR VICTORIE?
JUST SO YOU KNOW, I TASTE TEST ANY FOOD GIVEN TO MY SWEET VICTORIE. YOU CAN NEVER BE TOO CAREFUL!
WAIT, LACEY! THAT'S A--
PBBT
AHHH! GROSS!
NO WORRIES, LACEY. A MIX OF HONEY, LEMON, AND SNAKE SPIT WILL GET THAT STINK RIGHT OUT OF YOU!
YIP! YIP!
HISS!
END

WATCH OUT FOR PAPERCUTZ

Welcome to the seventeenth volume of THE LOUD HOUSE, from Papercutz, those wacky worker bees dedicated to publishing great graphic novels for all ages. I'm Jim Salicrup, the Editor-in-Chief, "El Jefe" of this crazy comics-creating company, here to ramble on a bit about the "Rule of Three."

Actually, and not really surprising, there are more than one Rule of Three. There's a Rule of Three that relates directly to comedy writing. Basically, it's creating a joke that's also called a "triple." The way it works is listing a few things, where a pattern is created by the first two things listed, and the third thing listed winds up breaking that pattern to comic effect. For example, if I listed the three most important meals of the day as breakfast, lunch, and snack time. Snack time, while certainly enjoyable, isn't necessarily an especially healthy or important meal, thus being included as such is a little surprising and therefore funny.

Other Rules of Three may refer to a grouping of three words, or three paragraphs, or even 3 graphic novels…

The Three Bears, The Three Musketeers, Three Blind Mice.

See no evil, hear no evil, speak no evil.

Even in the world of breakfast cereals, there's the Rule of Three...

Fans of ASTERIX (as well as Obelix, and Dogmatix), have probably seen our footnotes translating the Latin phrase, "Veni, vidi, vici," most often spoken by Julius Caesar, as "I came, I saw, I conquered." Well, not entirely, but that's another story.

Even the Declaration of Independence of the United States, you'll find our Rights include, "Life, Liberty, and the Pursuit of Happiness."

And one of our favorite ways to pursue Happiness at Papercutz is to enjoy graphic novels, which brings us to the various 3 IN 1 series that we proudly publish. There is also THE LOUD HOUSE 3 in 1 series that collects volumes just like this, featuring Lincoln Loud and the Loud family's antics and adventures. This is the man with a plan – or three – to stay on top in a house with ten sisters and lots of pets.

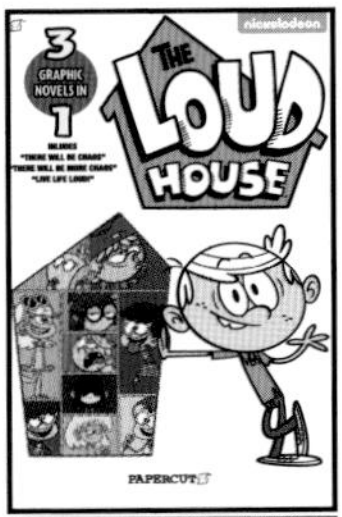

3 GRAPHIC NOVELS IN 1
THE LOUD HOUSE
nickelodeon

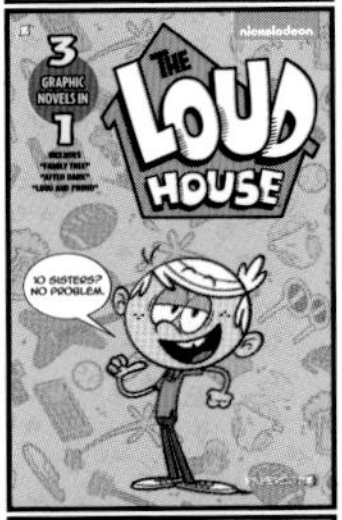

3 GRAPHIC NOVELS IN 1
THE LOUD HOUSE
nickelodeon
10 SISTERS? NO PROBLEM.

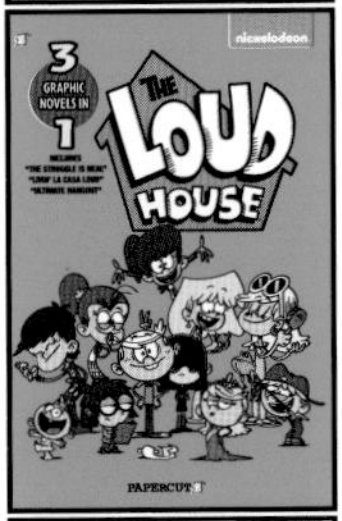

3 GRAPHIC NOVELS IN 1
THE LOUD HOUSE
nickelodeon

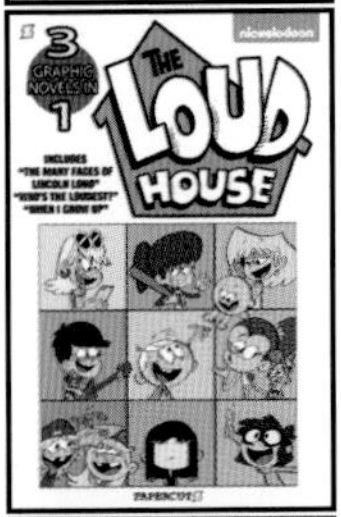

3 GRAPHIC NOVELS IN 1
THE LOUD HOUSE
nickelodeon

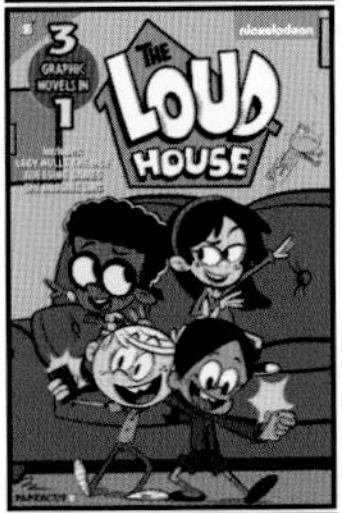

3 GRAPHIC NOVELS IN 1
THE LOUD HOUSE
nickelodeon

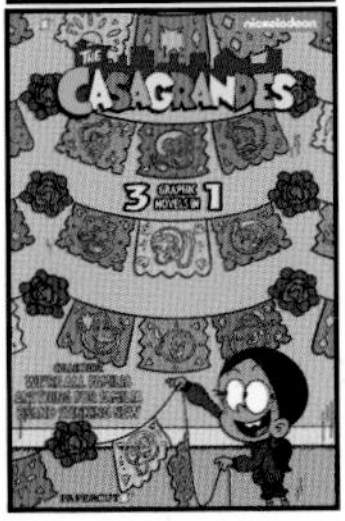

nickelodeon
CASAGRANDES
3 GRAPHIC NOVELS 1

While the previously mentioned ASTERIX graphic novel series isn't called ASTERIX 3 IN 1, it may as well be, as each volume collects three classic ASTERIX graphic novels, that Papercutz hadn't published individually. Likewise THE SMURFS TALES features three graphic novels by Smurfs-creator Peyo that hadn't been published by Papercutz before (with an exception or two), while THE SMURFS 3 IN 1 collects previously published Papercutz graphic novels of THE SMURFS.

The latest and greatest 3 IN 1 series are THE CASAGRANDES 3 IN 1 #1, which collects the first three graphic novels of THE CASAGRANDES and THE SISTERS 3 IN 1 #1 which, you may have already guessed, collects the first three graphic novels of THE SISTERS.

Also not surprisingly, variations of this very WATCH OUT FOR PAPERCUTZ column is appearing in three different graphic novels: THE LOUD HOUSE #17, THE SISTERS #8, and GERONIMO STILTON REPORTER #12. Hey, you wouldn't want me to break the Rule of Three, would you?

Thanks, Jim

STAY IN TOUCH!

EMAIL:	salicrup@papercutz.com
WEB:	papercutz.com
TWITTER:	@papercutzgn
INSTAGRAM:	@papercutzgn
FACEBOOK:	PAPERCUTZGRAPHICNOVELS
FANMAIL:	Papercutz, 160 Broadway, Suite 700, East Wing, New York, NY 10038

Go to papercutz.com and sign up for the free Papercutz e-newsletter!

nickelodeon GRAPHIC NOVELS AVAILABLE FROM PAPERCUTZ

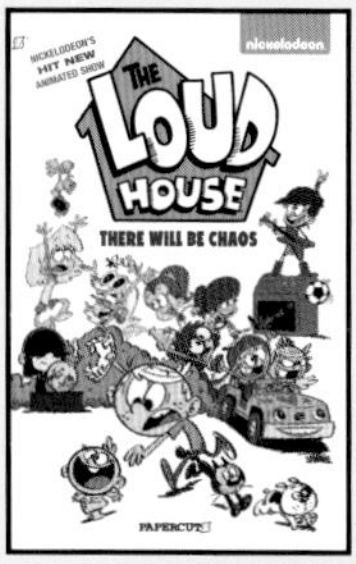
nickelodeon
NICKELODEON'S HIT NEW ANIMATED SHOW
THE LOUD HOUSE
THERE WILL BE CHAOS
PAPERCUTZ

THE LOUD HOUSE
#1
"There Will Be Chaos"

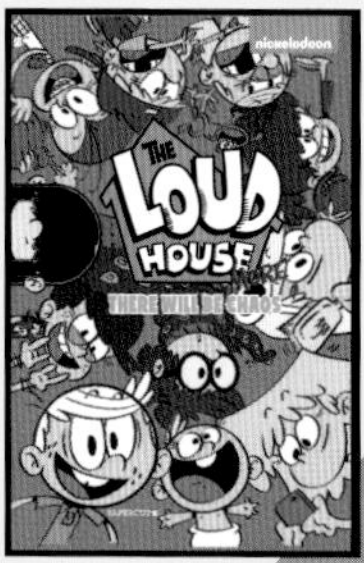
nickelodeon
THE LOUD HOUSE
PAPERCUTZ

THE LOUD HOUSE
#2
"There Will Be More Chaos"

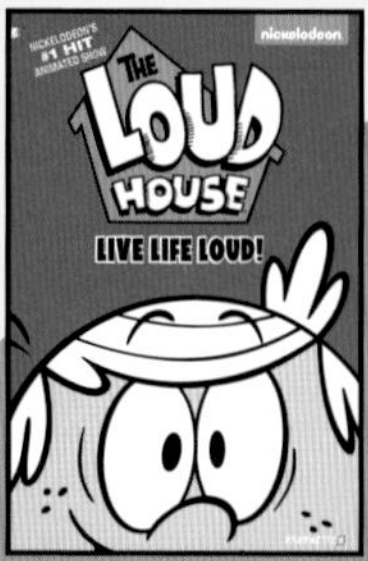
nickelodeon
NICKELODEON'S #1 HIT ANIMATED SHOW
THE LOUD HOUSE
LIVE LIFE LOUD!

THE LOUD HOUSE
#3
"Live Life Loud!"

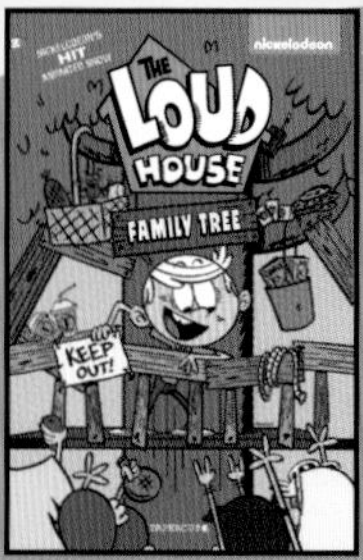
nickelodeon
THE LOUD HOUSE
FAMILY TREE
KEEP OUT!

THE LOUD HOUSE
#4
"Family Tree"

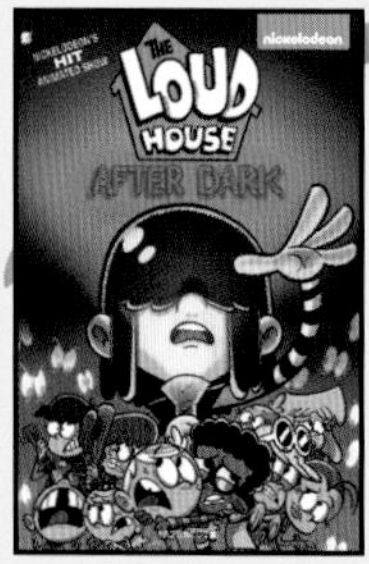
nickelodeon
THE LOUD HOUSE
AFTER DARK

THE LOUD HOUSE
#5
"After Dark"

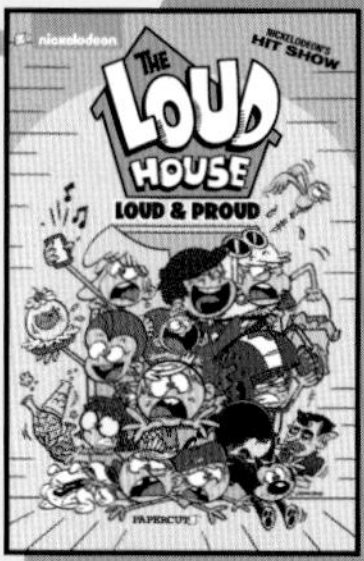
nickelodeon
NICKELODEON'S HIT SHOW
THE LOUD HOUSE
LOUD & PROUD
PAPERCUTZ

THE LOUD HOUSE
#6
"Loud and Proud"

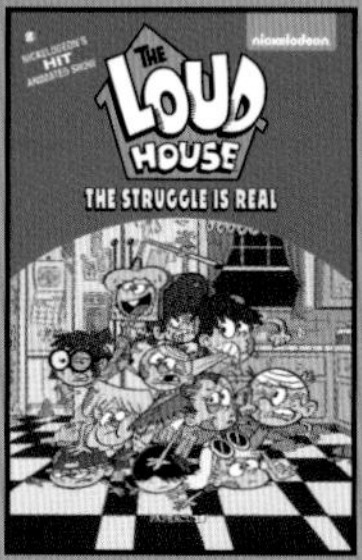
nickelodeon
THE LOUD HOUSE
THE STRUGGLE IS REAL

THE LOUD HOUSE
#7
"The Struggle is Real"

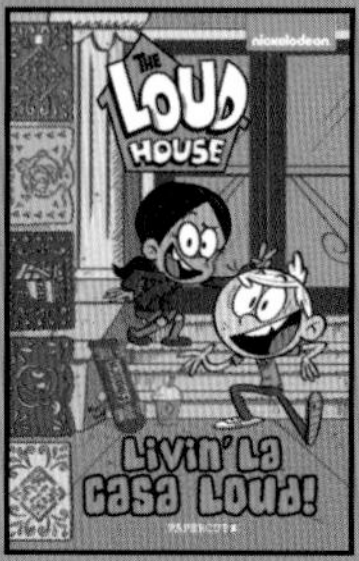
nickelodeon
THE LOUD HOUSE
Livin' La Casa Loud!
PAPERCUTZ

THE LOUD HOUSE
#8
"Livin' La Casa Loud"

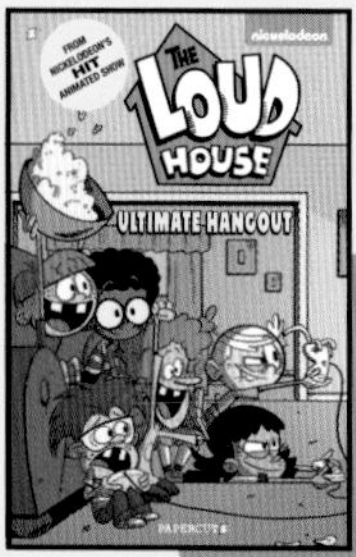
nickelodeon
THE LOUD HOUSE
ULTIMATE HANGOUT
PAPERCUTZ

THE LOUD HOUSE
#9
"Ultimate Hangout"

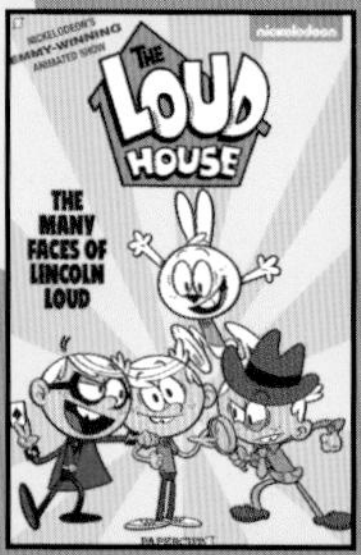
nickelodeon
THE LOUD HOUSE
THE MANY FACES OF LINCOLN LOUD

THE LOUD HOUSE
#10
"The Many Faces of
Lincoln Loud"

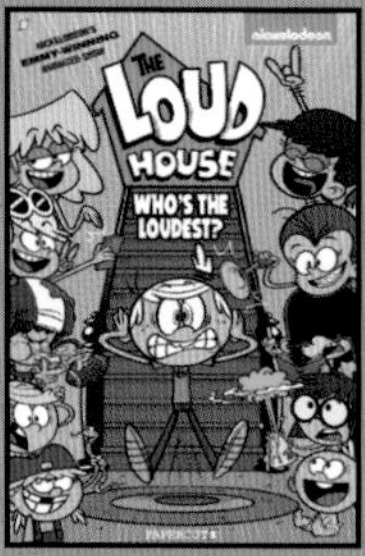
nickelodeon
THE LOUD HOUSE
WHO'S THE LOUDEST?

THE LOUD HOUSE
#11
"Who's the Loudest?"

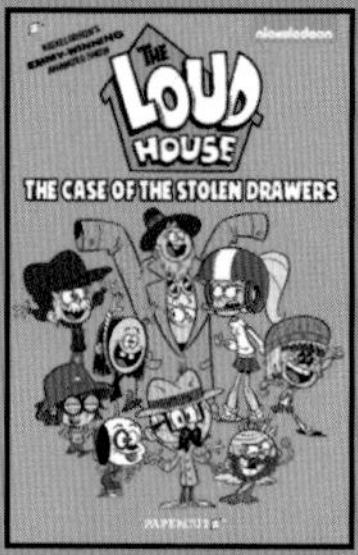
nickelodeon
THE LOUD HOUSE
THE CASE OF THE STOLEN DRAWERS
PAPERCUTZ

THE LOUD HOUSE
#12
"The Case of the Stolen
Drawers"

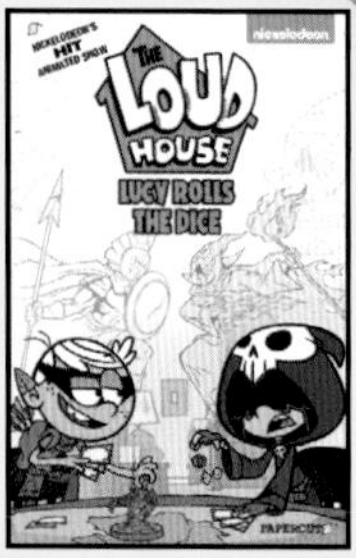
nickelodeon
NICKELODEON'S HIT ANIMATED SHOW
THE LOUD HOUSE
LUCY ROLLS THE DICE
PAPERCUTZ

THE LOUD HOUSE
#13
"Lucy Rolls the Dice"

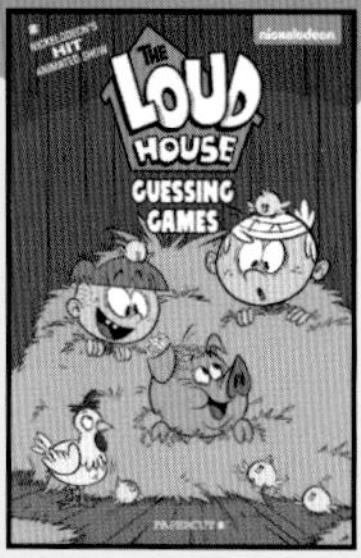
nickelodeon
NICKELODEON'S HIT ANIMATED SHOW
THE LOUD HOUSE
GUESSING GAMES
PAPERCUTZ

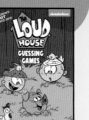

THE LOUD HOUSE
#14
"Guessing Games"

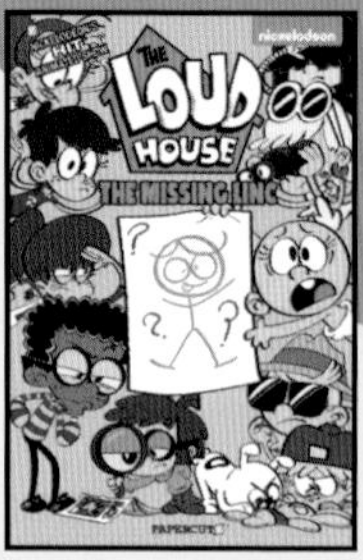
nickelodeon
THE LOUD HOUSE
THE MISSING LINC
PAPERCUTZ

THE LOUD HOUSE
#15
"The Missing Linc"

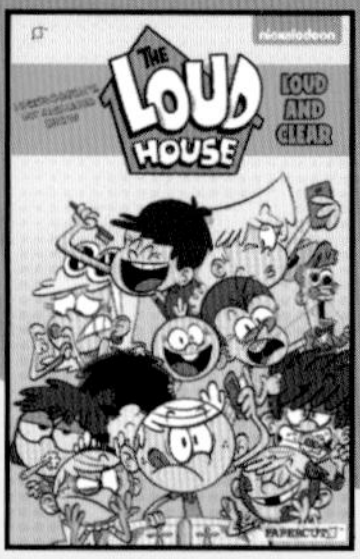
nickelodeon
THE LOUD HOUSE
LOUD AND CLEAR
PAPERCUTZ

THE LOUD HOUSE
#16
"Loud and Clear"

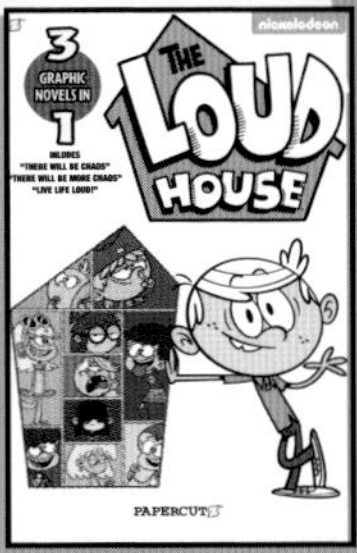
3 GRAPHIC NOVELS IN 1
THE LOUD HOUSE

THE LOUD HOUSE
3 IN 1
#1

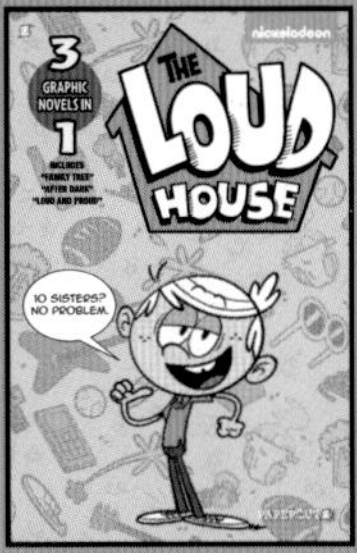
3 GRAPHIC NOVELS IN 1
THE LOUD HOUSE
10 SISTERS? NO PROBLEM.

THE LOUD HOUSE
3 IN 1
#2

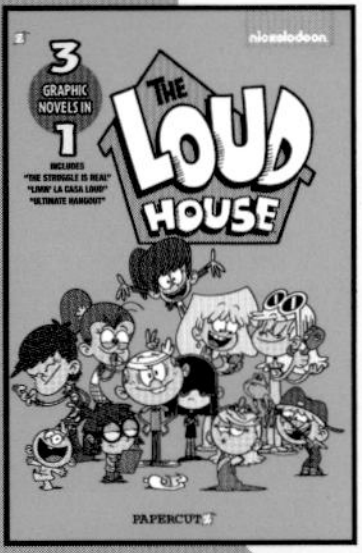
3 GRAPHIC NOVELS IN 1
THE LOUD HOUSE

THE LOUD HOUSE
3 IN 1
#3

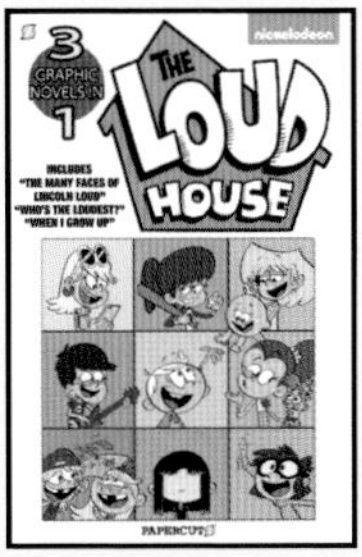
3 GRAPHIC NOVELS IN 1
THE LOUD HOUSE

THE LOUD HOUSE
3 IN 1
#4

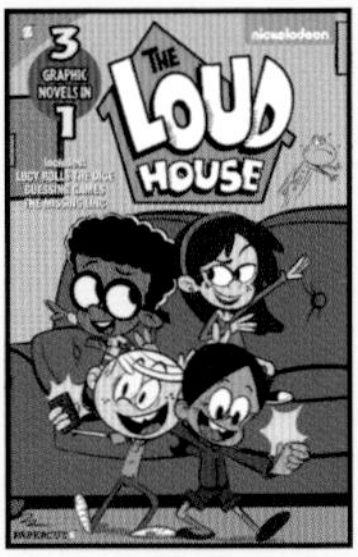
3 GRAPHIC NOVELS IN 1
THE LOUD HOUSE

THE LOUD HOUSE
3 IN 1
#5

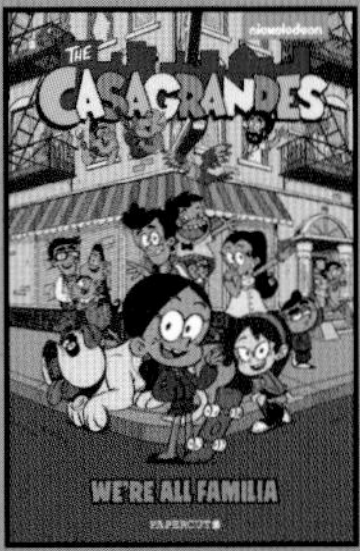
THE CASAGRANDES
WE'RE ALL FAMILIA

THE CASAGRANDES
#1
"We're All Familia"

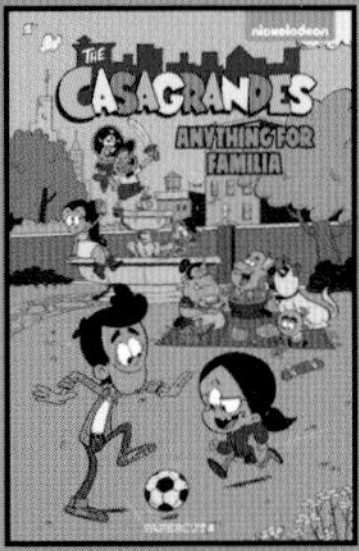
THE CASAGRANDES
ANYTHING FOR FAMILIA

THE CASAGRANDES
#2
"Anything for Familia"

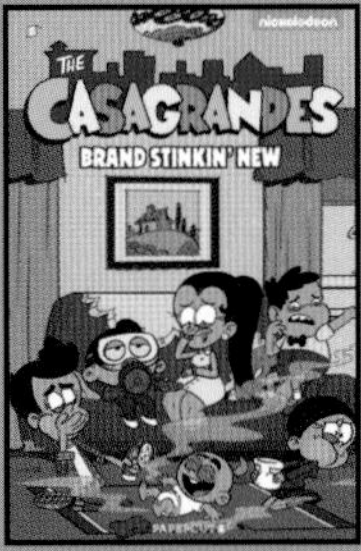
THE CASAGRANDES
BRAND STINKIN' NEW

THE CASAGRANDES
#3
"Brand Stinkin' New"

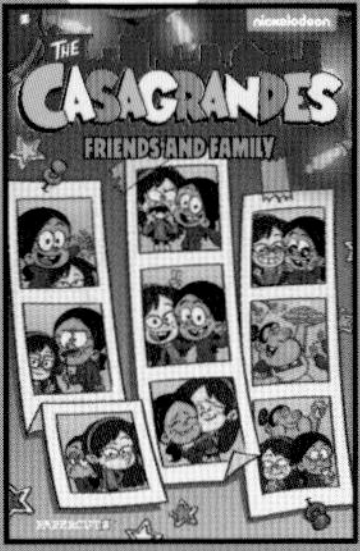
THE CASAGRANDES
FRIENDS AND FAMILY

THE CASAGRANDES
#4
"Friends and Family"

COMING SOON

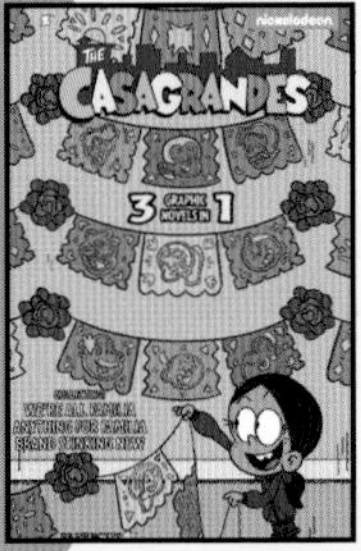
THE CASAGRANDES
3 GRAPHIC NOVELS IN 1

THE CASAGRANDES
3 IN 1
#1

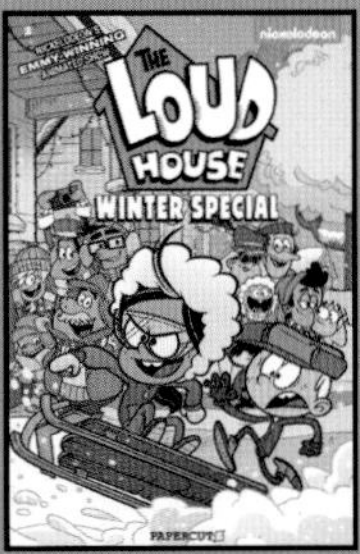
THE LOUD HOUSE
WINTER SPECIAL

THE LOUD HOUSE
WINTER SPECIAL

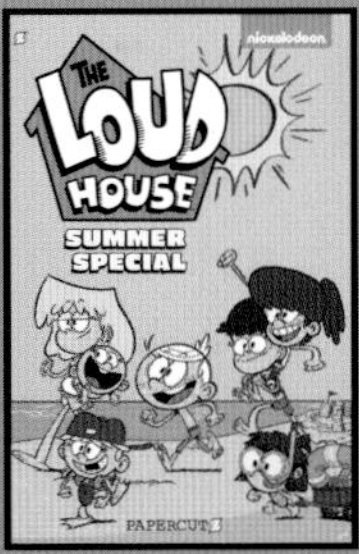
THE LOUD HOUSE
SUMMER SPECIAL

THE LOUD HOUSE
SUMMER SPECIAL

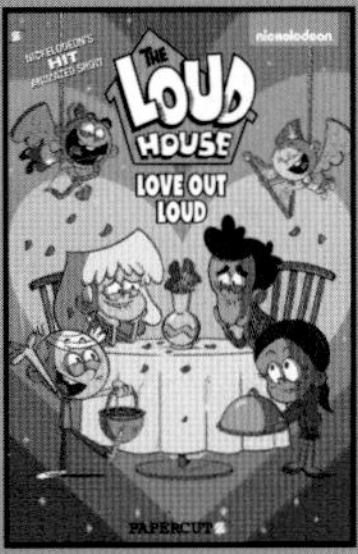
THE LOUD HOUSE
LOVE OUT LOUD

THE LOUD HOUSE
LOVE OUT LOUD
SPECIAL

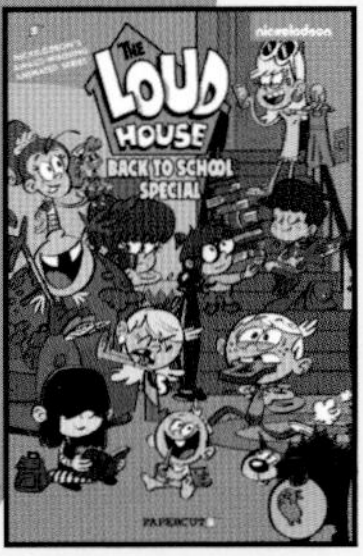
THE LOUD HOUSE
BACK TO SCHOOL SPECIAL

THE LOUD HOUSE
BACK TO SCHOOL
SPECIAL

COMING SOON

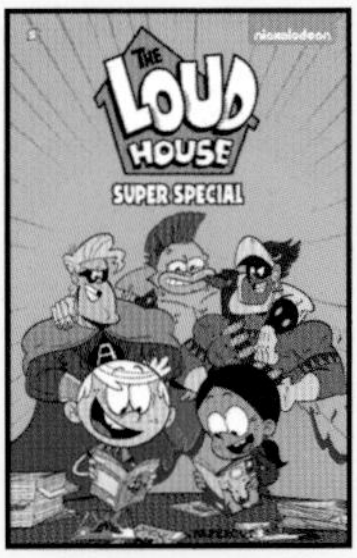
THE LOUD HOUSE
SUPER SPECIAL

THE LOUD HOUSE
SUPER
SPECIAL

THE LOUD HOUSE and THE CASAGRANDES graphic novels and specials are available for **$7.99** each in paperback, **$12.99** each in hardcover. THE LOUD HOUSE 3 IN 1 and THE CASAGRANDES 3 IN 1 graphic novels are available for **$14.99** each in paperback only.

Available from booksellers everywhere. You can also order online from Papercutz.com, or call 1-800-886-1223, Monday through Friday, 9-5 EST. MC, Visa, and AmEx accepted. To order by mail, please add $5.00 for postage and handling for the first book ordered, $1.00 for each additional book and make check payable to NBM Publishing. Send to: Papercutz, 160 Broadway, Suite 700, East Wing, New York, NY 10038.

Nickelodeon graphic novels are also available digitally wherever e-books are sold.

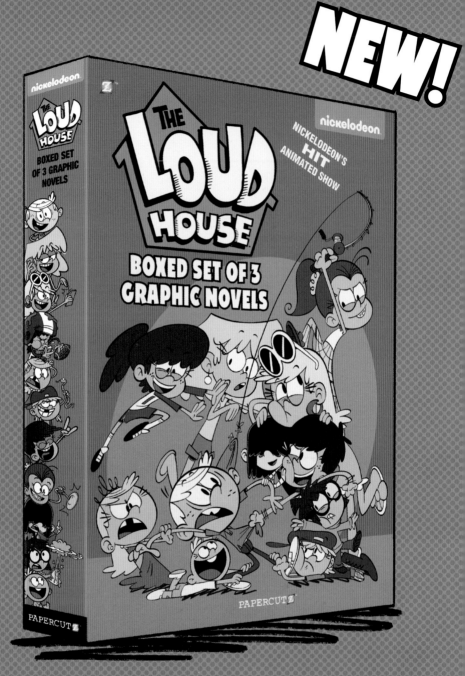